**"Emotion, li[...]
may swell. [...]**

Luis lowered his voice and continued, "Love between man and woman is like that, Laurel—one moment a placid stream, and then suddenly an overwhelming flood."

"Only to subside again, or dry up altogether," Laurel suggested in a strangled voice, recalling her sister and his brother.

"But left at full force it would eventually destroy the participants, and that would be such a waste.... Love should be enjoyed, Laurel, indulged in when it reaches its peak, before frustration sours it." He began to stroke her arm. "Laurel...." His voice was harsh with feeling.

"No!" she said sharply. She knew what he was going to say and didn't want to hear him say it. She longed for love between them, but he, being a man, thought only of consummation.

ELIZABETH ASHTON

is also the author of these

Harlequin Romances

Many of these titles are available at your local bookseller.

For a free catalog listing all titles currently available,
send your name and address to:

HARLEQUIN READER SERVICE,
1440 South Priest Drive, Tempe, AZ 85281
Canadian address: Stratford, Ontario N5A 6W2

White Witch

by

ELIZABETH ASHTON

Harlequin Books

TORONTO • NEW YORK • LOS ANGELES • LONDON
AMSTERDAM • PARIS • SYDNEY • HAMBURG
STOCKHOLM • ATHENS • TOKYO • MILAN

Original hardcover edition published in 1982
by Mills & Boon Limited

ISBN 0-373-02503-3

Harlequin Romance first edition October 1982

CHAPTER ONE

HAD she done the right thing by bringing Peter to Spain? Laurel wondered for the hundredth time, as she stood by the conveyor belt waiting for her luggage to appear. She was familiar with Malaga airport, she had stood in this very spot four and a half years ago, but in what different circumstances. Then she had been filled with eagerness to see her sister and her new baby, and was expecting Joanna's husband to meet her and take her out to his villa in Mijas where her welcome was assured. Now Pedro and Joanna were dead and she was bringing their son back to his father's people, not knowing who was going to meet her, that his grandmother, Doña Elvira, had not mentioned and she was doubtful about her reception when she did arrive.

She glanced at her watch, five a.m. Spanish time, an ungodly hour for any sort of rendezvous, and it was still dark.

The luggage was coming now, cases and holdalls of every shape and size, some new and expensive, others old and battered being seized by their impatient owners as they came within reach. Ah, there was her shabby brown one. She yanked it off the moving band.

'Where's mine?' Peter demanded, rubbing his

eyes. He had left the bench where she had told him to wait and crept to her side, fascinated by the moving traffic. Not yet five years old, fair-haired, blue-eyed, he looked wholly English, which Laurel feared would not endear him to his Spanish kin. He had his mother's colouring, and her late husband's people had every reason to resent Joanna.

She told him, 'It'll come soon.'

'There . . . catch it quick!' Peter yelled, lunging forward and nearly falling on to the belt. Laurel pulled him back with one hand as she reached for the small case with the other. A box containing the rest of his gear had been sent overland, for though her stay would be brief, his was to be permanent. She prayed fervently he would be happy with the Aguilas, and after all, he was one of them, though Joanna had reverted to her maiden name after she left her husband. Peter was by rights, Pedro Lester de las Aguilas—what a mouthful!—and he looked like a Saxon cherub.

She struggled towards the exit, a suitcase in each hand with Peter clinging to the edge of her loose jacket. She had nothing to declare except that she was weary and apprehensive, and she did not like airports, but that was of no interest to the stocky official watching them go through, who actually smiled as he met Peter's curious gaze.

Out into the forecourt, where the new arrivals were milling round trying to locate friends and transport, Laurel dropped her cases, wondering what to do next. She would have expected to have seen Pedro coming towards her, but in answer to her letter to him, telling of Joanna's death from a terminal disease, and her difficulties in supporting the child, his mother had informed her that Pedro, her middle son, had died in an accident a year previously, but they would be pleased to receive Pedro's son, and if she could bring him out, she must stay for a while until he had settled down in his new environment. The letter had been courteous but cold; Laurel could hardly expect it to be cordial when Joanna had persisted in concealing her whereabouts for over three years. She was obsessed with the fear that if he discovered them, Pedro would take her child away from her. Doña Elvira would think that Laurel had abetted her and only desperation had finally forced her to appeal to them. Joanna had been close as a clam about her married life, and Laurel had no idea of what had gone wrong. Any suggestion that she was being unfair to Pedro promptly sent her sister into hysterics.

Laurel gave a gasp and her eyes widened, as she caught sight of a tall man in a perfectly tailored grey suit pushing his way through the crowd towards her. The olive face with dark sideburns, the smooth black head and slightly arrogant bearing were familiar. Could it be that Pedro was not dead after all, or was she having an hallucination, evoked by her memories? Then she recalled that Pedro had had brothers, and this must be one of them, but the family likeness had given her a jolt.

He was staring at her intently as he approached, an enquiring, probing look, with a hint of suspicion, which she found disconcerting. He was assessing her and not liking what he saw. At close quarters the resemblance to his brother was less marked; he was taller, older than she remembered Pedro to be, and the mould of his face was stronger, almost harsh.

'Miss Lester, is it not?' He held out his hand—Spaniards always shook hands. 'I am Luis de las Aguilas.' Luis of the eagles, an appropriate name, for there was something hawklike about his keen profile and intent regard. 'I trust you had a good flight.'

Courteously spoken, but what an undercurrent of antagonism! Laurel barely touched the outstretched hand, gazing unsmilingly up into a proud, arrogant face, with eyes as hard and black as jet. This was the eldest brother, head of the family since his father died prematurely, who had set up the most virulent opposition to Pedro's runaway marriage. He had insisted it must be dissolved, and probably could have obtained an annulment as Joanna had not been a Catholic, and he had been trying to persuade Pedro to consent to it, when her pregnancy had scotched that charming idea. Joanna had spoken of him as if he were akin to the devil, but Laurel had not met him at the time of her previous visit, as he had been away. What on earth had induced him to come and collect them? Surely it would have been better to send a taxi? Laurel was prepared to hate him on sight, for she was convinced he had been instrumental in the breakdown of her sister's marriage. He had despised and resented Jo for being parentless and brought up in a home, facts which stuck in his snobbish gizzard. The prospect of a long drive in his company was anything but inviting, and if he thought he could intimidate her, he had another thing coming. Although she had been abandoned by her parents, she had made good, and was proud of her ability to earn her living, and was not going to show subservience to any arrogant Spaniard, however affluent he might be. She was here by his mother's invitation, and if he didn't like it, he could lump it!

'It was quite comfortable, thank you,' she replied with chill politeness, and saw his eyes had gone to her legs, and his lips curled in fastidious distaste. Laurel was wearing brown cords with a matching jacket, and she recalled that Joanna had told her that Spanish men disliked women in trousers. That was just too bad. She was not going to dress to conform with his old-fashioned prejudices.

His searching gaze returned to her face, lingering on her wide low forehead, vivid blue eyes and ash-blonde hair.

'You are very like your sister,' he said abruptly.

And that of course would not recommend her to him, who had so furiously resented Joanna.

'We have ... had, the same colouring,' she returned.

'But there is more character in your face, and you have honest eyes.'

What an odd thing to say—and was he going to keep her here all night, or rather morning for the night had passed, dissecting her appearance? Perhaps her similarity to Joanna had startled him, as his to Pedro had done her. That was understandable, but she couldn't help her looks and they were something else he would have to put up with. Probably he did not admire blondes, preferring the dark sulty beauties of his own nationality. That would not worry her, she didn't want his admiration. Although many men had found her fair, she preferred his disapproval.

'Thank you, but my honesty has never been in question,' she returned tartly, and he smiled sardonically.

She looked delicate and fragile beside his tall virile form, but her appearance was deceptive, because she was neither—she could not have coped with a job, an ailing sister and a small boy if she had been. All the same those years had taken their toll of her, she was too thin and there were violet marks under her eyes, increasing their size.

Luis's glance went from her to the boy.

'So this is Pedro, my nephew. He does not look as though he had a drop of Spanish blood in him.'

'Boys often take after their mothers.'

'In this case that is a pity.' His voice was very dry.

Peter stared up into his uncle's forbidding face.

'My name's Peter, and I'm Tia's nephew, not yours.' He took told of Laurel's hand. 'She's all

I've got now Mummy's gone to heaven.'

His lips quivered as he spoke of his loss, though he had not felt it very keenly. Joanna had spent the last months of her life in hospital and it was Laurel whom he loved and upon whom he depended.

Luis spoke to him in Spanish, and frowned at his blank look.

'He does not speak his own tongue?'

Laurel shook her head. That was not her fault, she only knew a few words of Spanish herself.

'But he called you Tia.'

'Jo used to refer to me as that to begin with, and somehow it stuck.

'A somewhat inadequate vocabulary,' he said sarcastically, then he noticed her pallor and heavy eyes and went on more kindly: 'I must not keep you standing here—come along to the car. You look very tired, and this is an unearthly hour to complete a journey.'

His English was unaccented, if a little precise. Jo had said his family all spoke it; it was their only virtue in her eyes.

Luis picked up their two cases and Laurel followed him out into the car park, still holding Peter's hand. He led them to what she saw without surprise—she was beyond being surprised by anything—was a Rolls, a Silver Shadow. She knew the Aguilas were affluent. Jo had brought a diamond necklace back with her; the sale of it had augmented Laurel's salary, and financed her medical bills.

Peter stopped and gaped at it.

'Is it all yours, mister sir?'

'*Por Dios*, do not call me that!' Luis exclaimed irritably. 'I am your Tio Luis; of course it is mine.' He opened the door to the front seat. 'Please to get in, Laurel,' he used her first name quite naturally. 'The *niño* can lie along the back seat and obtain the sleep he needs. You will remember it is a long drive to Mijas.'

She did, but when she had come before it had been daylight and she had enthused to Pedro about the beautiful country. He had been a much more genial character than his brother. She found the darkness depressing, for although it was May, Spanish time was ahead of British and the latitude much farther south.

Peter objected to this arrangement. He wanted to sit in front with Tia, he was querulous with fatigue.

'You will do as you are told,' his uncle said firmly. He picked up the small protesting figure and laid him on the back seat. Peter's bright head was nodding, and his eyelids half closed. As Luis with unexpected tenderness put a cushion beneath it and covered him with a rug, he was already asleep. Luis put their cases in the boot, then slid into the driver's seat, as Laurel asked anxiously:

'He won't roll off the seat, will he?'

'I think not. It is wide, and this car runs smoothly.'

Naturally it would, being what it was, and as he started the engine, she said politely:

'It is a magnificent car.'

'It is,' he said with satisfaction. 'I won it from a client at roulette.'

Laurel was surprised, since she had been told gambling was not encouraged in Spain. He seemed to guess her thought, for he explained:

'I do not often play, and this was in Monte Carlo. I was challenged by an oil-rich sheik, who was negotiating for land in Marbella, with more money than sense.' He laughed gleefully. 'He was unlucky.'

Laurel thought anyone would be who was foolish enough to tangle with Luis de las Aguilas. He would command even Lady Luck. She moved uneasily, aware of the atmosphere of hostily between them. He was a formidable personality, and the enforced intimacy of the car was oddly disturbing.

'Why was he buying land in Marbella?' she asked for the sake of something to say.

'We have a new Arab invasion there. Marbella will soon become a modern Granada. Ironic, when you think of all the effort needed to get them out of Spain at the time of the Catholic kings.'

'But weren't those Moors?' Laurel was vague about Spanish history.

'The same breed. Your sister made friends among them—unwisely so.' There was censure in his voice.

'I don't know much about her life out here,' Laurel confessed. 'She was a bad correspondent, and she wasn't in Spain long.'

'Long enough,' his tone was bitter. 'A pity she ever came.' He would feel like that, for he had considered Joanna was not good enough for his brother. She had been only eighteen when she had run away with Pedro, whom she had met at the wine importers where she worked. She had always been impetuous and headstrong, and the young Spaniard had been bewitched by her blonde beauty. At least he had married her, though the rashness of the whole proceedings had dismayed her sister.

'I agree with you,' she said quietly, 'since it didn't last, but she was very young and very much in love.' Luis gave a contemptuous exclamation. 'Oh, she was, and youngsters believe love lasts for ever.'

'You cannot be very much older. Are you equally impulsive?' he asked smoothly. 'If so, you may be something of a responsibility.'

She wondered if he were trying to be offensive, but she replied calmly: 'I'm a year older than Jo was, and I was always the practical one. I don't get carried away by my emotions.'

'That is something to be thankful for,' he said nastily. Definitely offensive! Laurel glanced at his handsome profile revealed from time to time by the street lighting. He resented her coming, that was obvious, and he was venting his disapproval of Joanna upon her innocent head, which was hardly fair. A proud, implacable Spaniard, she judged, with no sympathy for human weaknesses. Pride was a Spanish failing and Joanna had wounded the Aguilas'. He was hardly likely to find herself appealing.

Then she remembered that she was not the only one bereaved, he had lost a brother, and she ought to offer condolences. She said gently:

'I was so sorry to hear about Pedro's tragic accident. I ... I liked him, it came as quite a shock; we hadn't heard anything about him for a long time.'

'That was your sister's doing,' he returned shortly. 'She should never have married him. She hated Spain and disliked our way of life, and made no attempt to get on with the family.

'Who, I gather, didn't welcome her,' Laurel pointed out.

'My mother did her best, but they were not en rapport. We are a proud people and it was expecting too much of us to accept a foreign upstart without a dowry whose background was a charitable institution. Pedro inherited property, and we suspected her motives were mercenary.'

You would, Laurel thought angrily. 'That was utterly disproved when she gave up luxury for penury when she left him,' she declared, her voice quivering with indignation. 'As for the St Agnes' Foundation, it has turned out many worthy people, let me tell you. It was the only home we knew, and the staff were kind. You despise us for having no noble escutcheons, and you consider your brother made a mesalliance, but we were brought up to be virtuous, independent girls, which I'm sure is more than can be said for a lot of your fine ladies!'

They were travelling along the brightly lit streets which bordered the coast, the street lamps illuminating the interior of the car, and she saw his dark brows lift and a quizzical smile touch his lips. Involuntarily she noticed that he had a very handsome mouth.

'I cannot help my thoughts,' he returned courteously, 'but I was impolite to utter them. I apologise if I have offended you. May I say that I applaud your loyalty to your sister and the people who raised you. No doubt they deserve it, but she did not.'

'She's dead,' Laurel said wearily. 'Let her rest.'

'Certainly, but did you condone her action in depriving Pedro of his son, and keeping herself incommunicado for years?'

'Peter was all Jo had left,' Laurel tried to defend her sister. 'She was terrified Pedro would try to take him away from her.'

'He would not have done that. If she had applied for a separation she would have been granted custody while he was so young. All Pedro wanted was access to the boy.'

'Jo was certain that if he discovered her whereabouts he would try to kidnap the child. There have been many cases of that happening. It became an obsession with her as her health declined.'

Luis gave an exclamation of disgust. 'As if he would descend to such skulduggery! It never occurred to her that she was putting an intolerable burden upon you?'

'But it wasn't, we managed quite well . . . She sold her jewellery . . .'

'And did it never occur to you to ask how she got herself plus her jewellery and her baby out of Spain?'

'I did wonder,' Laurel told him, 'but she wouldn't tell me. She never would speak of her life here, so I've no idea what went wrong, but it must have been something pretty bad. They were so in love.'

'Infatuation,' Luis sneered. 'And it was bad.'

Laurel looked at him enquiringly, but he said no more.

'Was there another woman?'

Luis shrugged his broad shoulders. 'What if there was? Spanish women are expected to look the other way if their husbands stray. That is no reason to break a marriage. We do not marry for love, which you seem to think so important. The woman settles for a good establishment and it is her task to produce *niños*. What her husband does outside the home is not her concern.'

'What a deplorably chauvinistic attitude!' Laurel exclaimed, shocked by this cynicism. 'Are you married?'

'Not yet, but as I am head of the family it will be my duty to select a suitable wife. She will have a fine establishment, and of course she will be Spanish.'

'Of course,' Laurel echoed mockingly. So he had his eye upon some unfortunate *señorita* to run his home and bear his children while he came and went as his fancy beckoned. But she being his countrywoman would know what to expect, and perhaps in the long run the marriage would turn out more satisfactory than Joanna's passionate love affair which had ended upon the rocks.

'I'm not surprised Jo rebelled,' she said slowly. 'You see, she had a modern outlook, and so have I.'

'And permissive?' he asked slyly.

'Certainly not!'

'I am glad to hear that. Such conduct would not be tolerated here.'

As if her behaviour were anything to do with him! About to tell him so with vigour, she checked herself. She was to be a guest in his mother's house and he was Peter's uncle. She had better not antagonise him any further. She hoped fervently their contacts would be few to avoid ructions, for not only had his intolerant criticism of her sister infuriated her, but she was sure he had catalogued her as an equally undesirable person.

They had left the bright streets behind them and were following unlighted byroads. It was not yet light, and only an occasional wall or gateway showed up in the headlamps. Luis was a dark, slightly menacing figure beside her. It seemed they had been travelling for hours and the journey would never end.

She said quietly: 'Believe me, *señor*, I would not have written to Pedro if there had been any alternative. I had to be at work all day and the nursery school wasn't very satisfactory. As Peter grows older, his needs will increase, and I couldn't bear him to be deprived. I shall leave as soon as I'm satisfied he is happy here.'

Luis must not be allowed to suppose she meant to sponge on the Aguilas indefinitely.

'You are welcome to stay as long as you please,' he told her, but without warmth. 'In fact as you are a connection by marriage, it is our duty to care for you. Since you are alone in the world, I will make provision for you.'

'You will do nothing of the sort!' she returned fiercely, needled by this calm assumption of authority over her and his patronising tone. 'I don't want your . . . your charity, *señor*, I'm quite capable of earning my own living.'

A somewhat ungracious speech if his offer was kindly meant, but it seemed to amuse him.

'The independent British Miss,' he laughed. 'Nevertheless it is as well to have someone to fall back upon.'

But never you, with your lofty condescension, your obvious contempt. No doubt it would flatter you to have me grovelling at your feet for the few crumbs you were pleased to throw me, but I'd starve first! Aloud, she said stiffly:

'Thank you, but I'm sure the need will never arise.'

'At least you had the good sense to contact us upon Pedro's behalf, but why did you not do it before?'

'Behind Joanna's back? I couldn't do that.'

'Why not? It is what you should have done. *Bueno*, I appreciate your scruples,' as she was about to utter an angry denial. 'But before we leave this distressing subject, there is one question I must ask, and I hope you will give me a truthful answer.'

'If I can.'

There was a curious urgency in his tone and she wondered what was coming now.

'Has Peter, as you call him, ever had a serious illness?'

She wondered why that was important, as she replied:

'I assure you he's perfectly healthy, but yes, he had a very bad turn with measles and 'flu when he was three. We feared we were going to lose him, but he pulled through.'

'Joanna did not let his father know? She did not write to him?'

'Of course not. She was always terrified Pedro would employ a detective to trace her.'

'He was not all that anxious to get her back,' Luis told her drily. 'But he did want the boy. He considered it, but it was always *mañana* with Pedro, and he was killed before he did anything.'

But you are not one to procrastinate, Laurel thought, you didn't want the heir to your brother's property to be found, and you certainly didn't want to find Joanna. She asked probingly;

'My letter came as a surprise?'

'Yes, but we were all delighted to have news of the boy at last.'

He did not sound it. She ought not to have come, if he were going to be so inimical. His feelings towards herself were unimportant, but if extended to Peter could affect his wellbeing. Then she remembered how tenderly he had settled the tired child on the back seat and was reassured. Luis would never vent his spite upon a little boy.

'When did Joanna come to England?' he went on.

'Why, when she left Spain. Peter was a year old.'

Her mind went back to the night when Joanna had turned up at her bed-sitting room on the verge of a nervous breakdown, with a baby, a diamond necklace and not much else, demanding sanctuary. Laurel had with difficulty found a flat in another district to accommodate them. Later, when Jo had wanted to sell the necklace, she had asked her bluntly if it were hot, and Joanna had looked at her with reproachful eyes.

'I may be a bitch, Laurel, but I'm not a thief. It was a gift, bestowed upon me as . . . compensation.'

Compensation for what, and by whom—Pedro, or another?

'Of course she came to me,' she went on, 'I was her only living relative.'

Luis slanted a keen look at her. 'The trail led elsewhere, but it proved to be false.'

Laurel was silent. She didn't want to discuss her unhappy sister with this hard, unfeeling man. His manner changed.

'*Bueno*, I hope while you are here you will, as we say in Spain, consider my house is yours, though actually you will not be staying in my mother's house, but the hotel opposite to it. The Casa is not large and since the Reina Isabella is one of the many I own in Andalucia we often accommodate our guests there as an alternative. I myself have a suite in it. You will be very comfortable there.'

'I'm sure I shall.'

If an icy spray had been poured down her back, Laurel could not have felt more cold. So all the fine talk about being welcome meant nothing at all. Doña Elvira preferred not to have her under her own roof, did not want to admit her to her family circle—her, the despised daughter-in-law's sister, who would only be tolerated until Peter could do without her.

'And Peter?' she asked faintly. 'Are we to be separated?'

'Certainly not. He will share your room in the hotel . . . for the present.'

That was something, and she felt relieved. We're on appro, she thought wryly, until we have shown we're acceptable. At least, Peter is. I shall always be beyond the pale.

Apparently quite unconscious of the blow that he had dealt to her pride, Luis went on:

'Though it is a modern building, the Reina is designed like an old Spanish palace, it is very spacious and unusual.' He spoke with pride. 'My suite is on the floor above you, so I shall be able to keep an eye on you.'

'And make sure I don't disgrace you?' she asked coldly, still smarting from her exclusion.

'*Ay de mi*, but you are an English rose—with thorns!' he returned ruefully. 'You are determined to prick me, but I only meant I would ensure all was well with you.'

'I'm afraid I have a sharp tongue,' she said apologetically, 'but you'll agree my position is a little . . . difficult.'

'Only if you insist upon making it so,' he told her. 'Your sister has gone, and so has Pedro, and their problems died with them. We have a mutual interest in the *niño*'s welfare, so can we not all be friends, and please to call me Luis.'

This appeared to be an extension of the olive branch, and she returned: 'I would very gladly be friends, Luis.' But she had private reservations. She had been told it was impossible for a foreigner to divine what a Spaniard was really thinking. Luis had not attempted to disguise his contempt for Joanna, and his manner towards her until now had been critical and censorious. It was only as they approached his own domain that he had become more cordial, perhaps influenced by the Spaniards' ingrained hospitality, but she had a suspicion that it was only a mask, assumed for some devious purpose he wished to conceal. It was most unlikely there could be any genuine friendship between the product of an orphanage and the proud arrogant head of the Aguilas clan.

CHAPTER TWO

DAWN was breaking, the rugged crests of the mountains black against a grey sky, as the car surmounted the steep slope into Mijas and turned left towards the little town. Far below lights still twinkled in Fuengirola. Laurel remembered it all so well, the extensive view down to the sea, the arid slopes of the mountains to the east and north. There, upon a rise overlooking the road, was the red-roofed, whitewashed villa where she had stayed with Joanna and Peter had been born. She wondered who occupied it now. She had spent a very pleasant two weeks with the young couple, who could have foreseen that a year later her sister would turn up in her diminutive flatlet, plus baby but minus explanation? Her few letters—Joanna was a bad correspondent—had given no hint of impending catastrophe.

She remembered also seeing the hotel, as Luis turned off the main road and down a steep slope into the courtyard. It was a long low building; nobody in Mijas was allowed to erect more than three stories to deface the countryside, as did the towering concrete blocks along the coast, set in a terraced garden descending the hillside. Laurel could smell the roses; there were roses everywhere, already in full bloom. It was a delectable spot, a romantic spot, and yet Joanna's romance had failed.

You will do well to remember that, she told herself, but she could not imagine any liquid-eyed Spaniard sweeping her off her feet, as Pedro had Joanna. She was far too matter-of-fact, and she was so weary that all she could contemplate with enthusiasm was bed.

Luis got out of the car and went to ring the bell beside the imposing front door, which swung open at his summons, as if he were expected, as he probably was. He came back followed by a sleepy porter who collected their luggage, and unclicked her door, offering his hand to help her get out. She accepted it, for she was stiff with sitting and her legs felt as though they belonged to someone else.

His long, narrow hand felt very strong as it clasped hers, and she was aware of a tingle along her nerves at the contact. He looked unnaturally tall looming over her in the wan light—he *was* tall for a Spaniard, the average Andalucian being short and stocky. Must be some alien blood somewhere, she thought vaguely.

'Thank you,' she said politely, as she stood beside him on the paving, and she sensed his penetrating look.

'I believe you are a dangerous woman, Laurel,' he told her with an odd note in his voice.

She shook her head dumbly, too exhausted to ask his meaning. This was not the time to indulge in the sexual banter his remark seemed to demand, and he turned away abruptly to open the rear door. Lifting the sleeping Peter in his arms, he signed to her to follow. He paused on the threshold.

'*Bienvenida*, Laurel,' he said gravely.

Doubtless they say that to all the guests, she thought drowsily, as she stepped into the vestibule. Low-ceilinged, marble-floored, decorated with potted plants, this seemed to cover a vast area, the reception desk occupying one corner. Opposite the entrance, plate glass windows reflecting the concealed lighting revealed a flower-filled patio.

Luis turned right, through an archway, and right again down a long corridor, while a sleepy receptionist hurried after them, carrying a key. He unlocked a panelled door—all the rooms had massive wooden doors—and stood back to allow Laurel to enter, handing her the key.

'*Que duermas bien, señorita*,' he said courteously.

She smiled sweetly. To sleep well—she wanted nothing better. The porter followed with the luggage and dumped it on the racks provided for that purpose. Luis laid Peter down on one of the twin beds and fumbled in his pocket for a few pesetas. The man bowed and withdrew, while Luis turned to scrutinise the fair, flushed face upon the pillow. He's looking for some likeness to his father, Laurel surmised, but there was nothing in the child's features to connect him with the dark sardonic countenance bending over him, which belonged surprisingly to his uncle.

Luis straightened himself and looked at her. She braced herself, expecting some scathing comment, but surely it was not unusual for a boy to take after his mother, he must know that. She drooped, as pale and fragile looking as a snowdrop, while his searching gaze swept over her, but what he said was:

'You are very beautiful.'

Laurel started, and a flush like red wine ran up under her thin skin.

'I'm not—it must be the dim light, she told him, for the overhead bulb was not strong. 'I must be looking a mess after travelling all night, but perhaps you admire travel stains, *señor*?' She tried to speak lightly, for there was something in that intent regard that discomposed her.

'Luis,' he corrected her mechanically, still staring at her, a sensuous look in his black velvet eyes. Then abruptly he turned away towards the window, which was covered by a *reja*—the iron grille, a feature that was erected over all the lower windows of houses in that country. The room was on the ground floor, and a clump of red roses, regaining their colour in the strengthening light, grew outside it.

'Come here,' he beckoned to her.

Reluctantly she joined him, wishing he would go away and let her sleep. He indicated a square white house on the other side of the courtyard, a little to the left.

'That is my mother's house. You see, you are

practically part of it, and there was no need to feel offended.'

How uncannily he could guess her thoughts! She stammered: 'I wasn't . . . I'm not . . .'

He laughed softly. 'Do not pretend, Laurel.' He touched her cheek lightly with his fingertips. 'You are not really like Joanna at all.'

'She was prettier than I am.'

His face froze. 'Fair and frail,' he said acidly, 'but in spite of the evidence, I believe you are true.'

'I hope so,' she said uncertainly, wondering what on earth he was getting at and what he meant by evidence. 'I . . . I'm very tired, Luis.'

'I am being very thoughtless.' He drew the curtains over the window, shutting out the growing day. 'There is a house phone,' he pointed to it. 'Ring for anything you require. I will give orders that you are not to be disturbed until you are ready for your breakfast.'

But still he lingered, as if loath to go. Laurel moved purposefully towards her case, snapping open the hasps. It might be his hotel, but this was her room, and surely his Spanish sense of propriety should tell him he ought to get out of it. He seemed to have got the message, for striding to the door, muttering, '*Hasta luego*,' he went out, closing it softly behind him.

Laurel undressed Peter without waking him—nothing short of an earthquake would have done that—and slid him into bed. Then she looked about her. The room, a double one, was large, with two old-fashioned armoires on either side of the beds, containing wardrobes and drawers. A long shelf ran behind the beds. The bathroom was beside the door. She no longer felt sleepy and decided a bath would relax her. Seeping in the warm water, she thought about Luis de las Aguilas. She didn't want to think about him, for she had decided during that interminable drive from Malaga that she detested him, and would keep out of his way as much as possible, but he refused to be banished from her mind. He fascinated while he repelled and she could not deny his good looks. He was what her colleagues at the office would call a dreamboat, a dish, a rave or whatever was the latest in their absurd vocabulary to describe an attractive man, but she was convinced he had contributed largely to her sister's distress and had possibly engineered the breakdown of her marriage. Joanna had never been able to endure criticism and disapproval which he had obviously handed out by the bucketful, and he had had a lot of influence over Pedro.

'Oh, bother the man!' she exclaimed aloud, as she clambered out of the bath and dried herself with the thick white towels provided for her use. I hope one of his hotels falls down or catches fire and keeps him somewhere else, she thought. Peter's my job, I've got to help get him acclimatised, poor lamb, and no dreamboats, dishes or raves are going to distract me!

With which firm resolution she slipped into bed and fell asleep with the scent of roses wafting through the open window on the soft Andalucian air. Andalucia, the home of flamenco, serenades, and the passionate men and women of the south! No premonition warned her that she could fall a victim to its magic.

She awoke from a dream-haunted sleep in which a dark saturnine face predominated, to find sunlight streaming in through the chinks in the curtains and a tousled Peter sitting up demanding sustenance. She looked at her watch—after eleven, a preposterous hour to expect breakfast, but Peter must be fed. Tentatively she rang room service, asking if they could have something served in their room. After all, this was a hotel, not a private residence. The desk had received instructions and she was informed that *desayuno* would be coming *pronto*. She put on her dressing gown and drawing back the curtains looked across to the Casa de las Aguilas. It was fitted with the usual *rejas* over the lower windows and iron balconies in front of the ones above, and there was no sign of life. She started to unpack, for last night she had felt too tired to do more than find their night things. Peter was prancing about the room clad only in a pair of trunks.

'Why those bars over the window?' he demanded. 'Like a cage.'

'To keep intruders out.' Cage was an ominous simile.

'Why we not have them in England?'

'Because they are Spanish, but it might be a good idea, with so many thieves about.'

'Are things better here than at home?'

'Some things are, I expect.'

He called England home, but he would have to learn that he belonged to Spain. He looked so typically British that her heart contracted. Would he ever become reconciled to his heritage?

Breakfast arrived, brought by two obsequious waiters. There was orange juice made with fresh oranges, milk for Peter, coffee for Laurel, croissants, small cartons of preserves and honey, butter in silver foil, and a large bowl of fresh fruit. They were being accorded V.I.P. treatment. She saw the men glance curiously at Peter. They knew who he was, of course, and he was obviously not what they had expected.

'Say *gracias*,' she instructed him; he had better begin to learn the language.

'Gracious,' Peter responded obediently, and the waiters beamed at him.

'Why I say that?' he enquired when they had gone.

'It's Spanish for thank you, and it's *gracias*, not gracious.'

'Will I have to learn Spanish?'

'Don't you think it would be a good idea now you're in Spain?'

'No, 'cos I'd have to unlearn it when I go home.'

'It's always useful to know another language,' Laurel said carefully, again with that little pang. How could she tell the child that that rather forbidding house across the way was his home now, for presumably the Aguilas would take him into it eventually. Reminded of the family, she wondered what to wear, as presumably she would meet them shortly. They would expect her to be in mourning for Joanna, as they would be for Pedro, but the only black dress she had brought was a semi-evening dress, the rag she had worn for the funeral had been discarded. She compromised by wearing white, trousers and a sleeveless cotton top. Her very fair hair was almost silver, like frosted gilt, and the only colour about her was her vivid blue eyes and her red mouth. She would, she hoped, soon acquire a tan, her arms and neck were far too pale for this land of sunshine. Peter she dressed in shorts and tee-shirt, the latter out of deference to his Spanish relations; at home he could have run about without one.

A chambermaid came to do the room and realising with pleasure that she was not expected to make their beds, Laurel went with Peter out into the reception hall.

They descended marble steps marked 'To the Pool' and came to a sort of undercroft, on a lower level than the ground floor of the hotel. Glass doors gave access to a flat space in which was the swimming pool, surrounded by green lawn on which mattressed metal couches were arranged. Several guests lay upon them, grilling in the sun, only rousing themselves to lave their bodies with oil. Under the lee of the steep tree-clad bank that sheltered the grounds was a bar and tables covered by a trellis of creepers overhead. Here lunch would be served later on, but coffee and other beverages could be obtained at any time. On the opposite side, a balustrade divided the lawn from the descending levels of the gardens, with a view of the distant town and the sea, the skyscrapers in Fuengirola clearly visible. Behind the hotel and to the left of it was a rugged line of hills, the Sierra de Mijas. Peter was eager to explore and they went down flights of steps amid rockeries of flowering plants to discover a children's pool, a tennis court and other amenities.

'This is a nice place,' Peter declared. 'May I go in the big pool?'

'Presently,' Laurel told him, for she was expecting a summons from their hosts.

There Peter insisted he was hot, and stripped to his underpants, then demanded a Coke. While he was sucking it up through a straw, Laurel glanced up at the open balconies of the first floor, wondering if one of them were Luis'. As if she had summoned him, he came out of one of the rooms, arrayed in a multi-coloured towelling robe.

'Aren't you going to swim?' he called. 'I am.'

He disappeared before she could confess that she had never learned that art.

He reappeared through the lower doorway, his robe over one arm, and a couple of towels, clad in black swimming trunks. The whole of his bronzed body was exposed and Laurel felt her pulses stir, because it was beautiful. Lean muscular chest without hair (did he shave it?), slim waist, long graceful legs. He dropped the gear he was carrying, and stepping to the side of the pool, dived in, shooting the length of it in an underwater crawl.

'Ooh, I'd like to do that!' Peter gasped.

'And so you shall.' Luis came up beside them, his wet black head like that of a seal. 'Come on, I will give you a lesson.'

Peter shrank back and Laurel put a protective arm around him.

'He can't swim.'

'Then of course he must learn. Jump in, *chico*, I will hold you.' Peter shrank even closer to her. '*Madre de Dios!* An Aguilas and afraid of water!'

''Course I'm not,' Peter declared, and ran to the edge of the pool.

'No!' Laurel cried, while a cold shiver ran down her spine, in spite of the hot sunshine. When Luis had mentioned Pedro's property, she had been too preoccupied to take in the full implication. By Spanish law all children inherit equally and Pedro would have obtained a large share of his father's estate, and it was to Joanna's credit that she had never made any claim upon him, but his brothers stood to lose with Peter's advent—was that why Luis had enquired about his health? If he wanted to dispose of him an easy way had presented itself. The pool was deep, the shallows did not extend far, and she could not plunge in to the rescue, she would only drown herself.

Ignoring her protest, Luis reached up and took hold of the little boy, lowering him gently into the water.

'Ugh . . . it's cold!' Peter spluttered.

'It only feels so at first.' Standing up to his waist in water, Luis supported him, urging him to strike out and kick. Peter, with his face set in grim determination, strove to follow his instructions.

'You won't let me go?' he asked anxiously.

'You can trust me.'

Peter began to enjoy himself, he laughed and splashed. He had a natural aptitude and made quick progress, having complete confidence in his teacher. He objected strongly when Luis told him he had had enough for a first time, and lifted him on to the pool's edge at Laurel's feet. The intensely black eyes met hers with a mocking glint, as if he had divined the reason for her perturbation.

'I am not the wicked uncle of the fairy stories,' he told her, and Laurel turned her head away in shame, disturbed that he seemed able to read her thoughts.

'What an idea!' She tried to brazen it out, and he smiled ironically.

'*Your* idea. Like your sister, you have a vivid imagination.'

Peter intervened, demanding to go in again.

'Tomorrow,' Luis told him. He again looked at Laurel. 'Too cold for you?'

'Tia can't swim,' Peter informed him.

'Is that so?' Luis drawled. He reached for his towels and threw one to Peter. 'Then tomorrow you can both have a lesson.' His eyes raked Laurel's figure as if he were envisaging her in a swimsuit, and she felt her colour rise. She did not blush easily and she was furious with herself for being so discomposed by a man she was determined to dislike.

'Thank you,' she said disdainfully. 'I'd hate to put you to so much trouble.'

'No trouble at all, it would be a pleasure, *señorita*.'

Oh, will it? she thought savagely, imagining those strong brown arms supporting her flailing limbs. He would enjoy having her at his mercy, no doubt. At the same time she felt a little thrill of excitement. He undoubtedly had something, this dark Spaniard, and he was affecting her strongly against her will. It must be the same magnetism that had caused Joanna to go off the deep end about his brother, which until now she had been unable to understand, the call of the dark blood to the fair. But as she had told him, she was the practical one of the sisters, and she had no intention of falling under the spell of this Don Juan, for that was what he was, who took ex-marital infidelity as a matter of course. Even if they were married, she would never be sure of him. Married? Was she crazy? But didn't every young girl subconsciously regard every attractive male she met as a possible husband, though she considered herself long past such juvenile folly. In all the wide world there was no more unsuitable mate for her than Luis de las Aguilas, and she was sure he would heartily agree with her.

The waiters were starting to bring out the luncheon dishes, laying them out in the covered tables in front of the bar. There was a multitude of succulent confections from which the visitors could help themselves to whatever they fancied.

Their advent proved a distraction from swimming. Luis swung himself out of the pool, and Peter, eyeing the convoy hopefully, announced:

'I'm hungry!'

'You've only just had breakfast,' Laurel reminded him, drying him vigorously with Luis' spare towel.

'Swimming makes you hungry, doesn't it, mister?' He looked up appealingly to his tall uncle, who was using the other one.

'Tio to you,' Luis corrected him. 'It certainly does, and you shall choose whatever you fancy.'

'He'll make himself sick,' Laurel protested, redressing him in his shorts, minus his underpants. She was glad to turn her eyes away from Luis' near-nakedness. Pedro had been a handsome man, but his brother was more so, he had a finer physique, and carried himself more proudly. She thought inconsequently: For God's sake cover yourself up, man, I'm not used to so much masculine glamour!

'He'll think it worth it, and there are plenty of people to clear up after him,' Luis said carelessly, as he put on his beach robe, but that wasn't much better. Swathed in its rich colours, he looked like an Eastern prince.

Most of the loungers were occupied, but with a

flick of his fingers, Luis had the attendants running to produce two more with their mattresses,
which they set up at the spot he indicated half in
sun and half in shade. There was no doubt who
was master at the Reina Isabella. Laurel sat down
on one of them with Peter beside her; Luis
stretched himself on the other one, and when a
waiter came hurrying up, ordered iced drinks.

'Sangria for you and me, orange for Pedro.'

'My name's Peter,' the child objected, 'and why
can't I have san . . . what you said?'

'Because if it includes brandy, as it will for me,
it is too strong for you—and your name is Pedro
now you are in Spain.'

Some recollection stirred in the boy's mind.

'It was Daddy's name, wasn't it?'

'Yes. It is something that you know that much.'
Luis' tone was sarcastic.

'Mummy never would talk about him,' Peter
complained. 'Was he dark, like you?'

Luis said he was.

'I wish I was dark,' Peter evidently admired his
uncle. 'But I'm like Tia.'

'Very like.' There was a peculiar inflection in
Luis' voice. 'But do not despair, darkness may
descend upon you as you grow older. I have
known blonde babies turn into brunettes, and I
think I detect the beginning of the Aguilas nose.'

That, Laurel thought, was a flight of fancy,
Peter's nose was as yet unformed, but it was nice
of Luis to humour the child. He had positioned
himself so that he had a clear view of her, and she

fidgeted under the watchful gaze from those black
eyes. What was he looking for, she wondered,
some evidence of lowly origins so that his contempt for the Lesters could be fully justified?
Thank goodness nature had been generous to her
in that respect. Her bone formation was elegant,
her wrists, ankles and hair were as fine as those of
any blue-blooded aristocrat. Only her mother had
known who her father was, and she had vanished;
he might have been a duke or a dustman. When
they were little Laurel and Joanna had played a
childish game, pretending they were the offspring
of princes, and no one could disprove their fantasy, with any certainty. It must gall Luis' pride
to know they had been waifs and strays, for the
Aguilas were highly conscious of their own ancient lineage. All a lot of nonsense, she thought
scornfully; it was what men or women made of
themselves that mattered, not what they were
born.

The waiter brought their drinks, and when he
had departed, Luis asked:

'What is troubling you now, Laurel?'

Oh dear, she thought, there it was again, that
mental rapport that she found so disconcerting.

'Nothing,' she returned, 'what makes you think
I'm upset?'

'Your cheeks are pink and your eyes have an
ireful sparkle. Is it because you think I wanted to
drown Pedro, and am now plotting to poison him
with rich food?'

'Oh, don't be so ridiculous!' she cried, flushing,

knowing he had guessed what she feared beside the pool, and how absurd that fear now seemed.

Luis laughed low in his throat; what a sexy laugh he had, Laurel thought wildly, as Peter exclaimed indignantly:

'He was teaching me to swim. You must be crazy, Tia!' He seized Luis' hand. 'Can we go and choose our grub now?'

Luis raised an interrogative brow. 'Grub, nephew?'

'Don't you know that means eats?'

'Oh, does it?' Luis rose languidly to his feet. 'Then come along, infant,' he slanted a wicked glance at Laurel, 'we will select your poison. Can I bring you anything, Laurel?'

'No, thank you,' she replied haughtily. 'I'm not hungry.'

'It is a long time until dinner.'

'I may help myself to something later on, they don't clear away until two o'clock.'

'She does not trust me,' Luis complained to Peter as they moved off.

And why should I, she thought, when all I know about you is that you hated poor Joanna and did your best to get rid of her? You say I'm very like her, so you probably hate me too under that suave façade you use to disguise your feelings. Was that the meaning of his continual staring? The thought was painful. Oh, damn him, she told herself angrily, I don't care what he thinks about me—but, inconsistently, she did.

When they returned Luis was carrying two

plates, one of which he handed to her together with the necessary cutlery, wrapped in a paper napkin.

'Stuffed avocados,' he told her. 'Peter said you could not resist those. They are one of the hotel's specialities.'

His own plate was heaped with paella.

Laurel felt ashamed of her previous hard thoughts.

'You're too kind,' she exclaimed impulsively. 'I don't deserve such generous treatment.'

He gave her an enigmatical look.

'Fortunately for us, we do not always get what we deserve,' he drawled.

Laurel looked away from the tall figure wrapped in his brilliant robe. Luis was altogether too attractive.

'Doesn't Señora de las Aguilas want to see her grandson?' she asked, changing the subject.

'Very much so. She will receive you after her siesta. She thought you would wish to rest this morning.'

Laurel revived her recollections of the small, formidable woman whom she had met in Joanna's villa. She had been courteous but aloof—disliking them both, Laurel had thought; only her eagerness to see her grandson had induced her to enter the house. It was Peter she wanted now, and Laurel hoped fervently that they would take to each other, for until Luis took a wife, she would be the dominant female influence in his life.

'My sister Mercedes and my young brother are

also at home,' Luis went on, 'and anxious to meet you.'

'How nice,' Laurel murmured faintly. So she was going to have to face the whole clan, who would probably be hostile and certainly critical. 'I . . , I'm shy of strangers.'

'They are not strangers, but your relatives,' Luis told her repressively.

Not mine, but Peter's, she reflected, and I do hope he makes a good impression. She glanced affectionately at the fair head bent over his plate of various fish and meat concoctions chosen from the laden buffet. If only he were her own and she could keep him with her, but these superior Aguilas were his kin, their blood ran in his veins, though looking at him it was hard to believe it. They would give him all the advantages that he deserved—a good education, fine clothes, good food far beyond anything she could have done for him, who could only give him love. It was strange that Joanna had no qualms about denying him his birthright, but Joanna had never looked ahead, or been unselfish concerning others. Peter was her baby, and she meant to keep him, until, when she knew she was dying, she had told Laurel to contact his father. Well, here they were, and soon she would be expected to fade out, leaving him to their tender mercies, which she prayed *would* be tender.

'Now you look pensive,' Luis broke into her thoughts. 'The family cannot eat you, and they *are* the family.'

'Which means nothing to me,' she sighed, 'never having had one.'

He looked almost sympathetic. 'That was a great hardship.'

'Oh, I don't know. Lots of families squabble dreadfully, so I've been spared that. In any case, I'll soon be going . . .'

'No!' Peter cried shrilly. 'You mustn't leave me, Tia, ever!'

They had forgotten him. Laurel could have kicked herself for her thoughtlessness, forgetting he could overhear. Leaving his unfinished plateful, Peter was clinging to her, his eyes wide and fearful.

'It's all right, darling,' she soothed him. 'I'll still be here. I won't go as long as you need me.'

Over his bent head she caught Luis' sardonic eye.

'Then you had better reconcile yourself to a long stay,' he told her.

CHAPTER THREE

As it would be quite late in the day when Laurel met the family, she changed into her filmy black dress. It had long loose transparent sleeves, and was midi-length. It emphasised her extreme fairness, and made her thin skin look translucent. I don't look too bad, she thought as she surveyed herself in the long glass on the wall. Peter in white silk shirt and shorts was excited, and deluged her with questions.

'Will Granny be nice? Is she very old, does she use a stick? Will she like me?' he demanded. 'Oh, there's Uncle Luis,' as a knock came on the door, Luis had said he would collect them. He flew to open it, and Laurel went slowly to join him.

Evidently he treated his mother with ceremony, for he was wearing a white dinner jacket over dark trousers, freshly shaved, his black hair slicked down over his scalp, and he looked devastatingly attractive. He spoke to Peter, who ran on down the corridor, and as he turned his head to look at Laurel standing beside him, he caught his breath and his eyes kindled.

'Are you real?' he asked. 'You look as insubstantial as a fairy, some enchantress out of legend.'

'Of course I'm real,' she laughed. With unconscious provocation in every line of her slight body, she held out her arm to him. 'Pinch it and you'll find I'm solid!'

'You deserve a more romantic approach than a pinch,' he responded, with a deep note in his voice. He put his hands lightly on her shoulders to draw her nearer, and bending his haughty head, touched her lips.

The contact of his mouth on hers acted like a match to tinder. A sudden upsurge of primitive passion exploded between them, engulfing them in its flame. Luis' hands dropped from her shoulders and he enfolded her in a constricting embrace. His mouth pressed deeper and deeper into hers, forcing her lips apart. Far from her resenting this treatment, Laurel's arms crept round his neck, and her limbs seemed to become fluid as she pressed herself against him. Time stood still while they were lost in a flood of rapturous sensation. Then Luis' hold relaxed, and he removed her clinging arms, pushing her almost violently away from him, while he muttered something in Spanish including the word *loco*, which meant mad.

Laurel swayed and clung to the handle of her door for support, for her legs were trembling. She had often been kissed before, what attractive modern girl had not, but she had never cared for amorous dalliance, and her boy-friends had called her cold. She had no idea a male embrace could so strongly affect her. She had been aware from the first of a physical attraction between them though she had heartily disliked him. That it could become so overwhelming gave her a shock. She looked at Luis and saw he was white and shaken. He too had been taken by surprise by the force of their mutual emotions. With an effort he pulled himself together, and looked at his watch.

'We will be late.'

The casual observation incensed her, no apology, no excuse, and she was feeling shattered. Were such incidents commonplace to him?

'That can't be helped. I'll have to repair my make-up.'

She opened the door and escaped into the sanctuary of her room. Was that the meaning of all those questioning glances? Luis de las Aguilas had merely been wondering if she were available. With his low opinion of the Lester girls, he would see no reason to respect her. With trembling fingers she wiped her smudged mouth, but she did not attempt to repaint it, her hand was shaking too much.

Men made passes at girls, it was the nature of the beast, but what had shaken her was her instantaneous response. She had never dreamed she was capable of such wanton behaviour. She should have slapped his insolent face instead of returning his kisses. What must he think of her? Probably that she was a common little tramp. And yet . . . And yet . . .

She had a suspicion that Luis had only meant to make a gallant gesture, and he had been taken as much by surprise as she had been by the upsurge of physical desire that had overwhelmed them. Latin men were emotional and amorous, but she, the cool Northerner, should have had more self-restraint. Red roses, hot sunshine, blue skies and Luis' black eyes had bewitched her. This was Spain that had brought disaster to her sister and would do the same to her if she didn't watch her step. For there could be no greater mismatched couple than herself and Luis de las Aguilas, the eagle and the dove, and the dove was lucky if it escaped with only a wounded breast. She did not think he would pursue her further, he had only yielded to a violent impulse aroused by her foolish invitation. She must be very careful in future to avoid any physical contact now she knew how dangerous it could be, and she was confident he would co-operate for he could no more desire an affair with her than she did with him. Perhaps he would take himself somewhere else for the duration of her stay, and she was dismayed by the desolation this idea caused her.

'Even so, quickly may one catch the plague.'

But she hadn't fallen in love with Luis, far from it, love had nothing to do with the turmoil of emotion that had sprung up between them. Love, true love, couldn't be born so quickly, whatever the poets said. Love was mutual trust and understanding, and she neither trusted nor understood Luis; she wasn't sure she even liked him. She must be the victim of a sudden infatuation, though that wasn't quite the right definition. But she mustn't stand here forever trying to analyse her feelings, he was waiting to take her to be

introduced to his formidable family, and they
would be a salutary tonic, for they would only
tolerate her for Peter's sake, and would be thankful to see the back of her. Among his own people
the gulf between her and Luis would be emphasised.

It was a very dignified, very cool and very self-
possessed Laurel Lester who finally came to
rejoin Luis, who had taken himself off to the reception hall, where an impatient Peter kept demanding where had Tia got to.

Luis' dark face was inscrutable as she came up
to them, and he remarked casually:

'I have been telling my small nephew he will
have to accustom himself to waiting for the ladies
he is going to escort.'

'But Tia never keeps people waiting,' Peter
protested.

Laurel smiled wanly. 'Sorry, Peter, I had a
slight mishap.' She shot Luis a venomous look.
'But the damage is repaired now. Let's go.'

But wasn't the damage irreparable?

The Casa de las Aguilas was approached by a
flight of steps leading up to a massive oak door,
which opened into a vestibule full of potted
plants, including the now despised aspidistra,
which seemed to be a favourite in Mijas. Indoor
plants appeared to be a feature of Andalucian
decoration. The *salón* was a square room with
french doors opening on to a small patio, three
walls of which were covered with flowering plants
in little pots suspended on them, the fourth being

draped in a pink ivy geranium. A fountain threw up a jet of water in its centre.

Doña Elvira de las Aguilas y Mendoza, to give her her full name, for Spanish women retained their maiden names attached to their husbands', though they were never addressed by them, was seated in a throne-like armchair beside the empty fireplace. Her small rotund figure in heavy black reminded Laurel of the pictures of Queen Victoria, but her face with its high-bridged nose was thinner and sharper. Mercedes, her firstborn, was tall and thin, very plainly dressed, her only ornament a silver cross hanging about her neck. Esteban, the youngest, was a lively-looking young man, very like his brothers, but with brown eyes instead of black. Since all her children were so tall, Laurel concluded they had inherited their height from their father, and she subsequently discovered he had been a big man, his mother being a strapping Austrian, who boasted of Hapsburg blood.

Laurel was formally presented to each in turn, and they all greeted her courteously, the women kissing her cheek, Esteban shaking her hand, without betraying the thoughts behind their opaque eyes, but she was conscious of undercurrents. Doña Elvira made Peter sit by her side, offering him sweets from a box on a small table beside her.

'You like the bonbons, *si*?' The child nodded shyly. She said something in Spanish and he looked blank. '*No comprendo?* That is bad.' She looked accusingly at Laurel.

'His mother always spoke English to him,' Laurel told her.

'Ah, *si* . . . his mother!' Elvira sucked in her lips disapprovingly and exchanged glances with Luis.

Peter caught sight of a bundle of hair in a basket by the hearth; the room had an old-fashioned grate disguised by a jar of flowers.

'A doggie!' he cried delightedly. 'May I stroke it, please, Granny?' A small black poodle had raised its head.

'My Pom-pom? Yes, if you are gentle—but you must call me Abuela.'

'Why?'

'Because that is Spanish for grandmother. *Ay mi*, you are your mother's child entirely! I see nothing of my Pedro in you.'

Mercedes said something in Spanish and Luis answered her in the same tongue. Both of them looked towards Laurel, who was sitting near the entrance to the patio, feeling very much an outsider. Sunlight pouring through the glass gilded her hair; nervousness had brought rose petal colour to her cheeks, and intensified the blue of her eyes. Her white fingers were clasped about her crossed knees, and her black drapery fell softly to the floor. She looked like a white dove in a flock of rooks among the dark Spaniards. Esteban, obviously smitten, broke into an impassioned torrent of speech, and Laurel surmised that Mercedes had said something derogatory. Luis smiled with tolerant amusement at his young brother's championship, but their mother cut him short with sudden asperity.

'*Basta*, it is enough. Is this the way to greet a guest? Is it polite to speak a language she does not understand? Esteban, ring the bell for Manolo, we will take refreshment now.'

The arrival of a manservant carrying a tray loaded with drinks and *tapas*, little savoury pieces, prawns, cheese, olives, etcetera, broke the strained atmosphere. Laurel refused wine, but accepted coffee. Esteban pulled up a stool to sit at her feet, his liquid brown eyes expressing unutterable things, the sum of which meant bed, but that was the way Spanish youths looked at girls they admired. Pom-pom, with canine cunning, decided that Peter was the best bet for titbits, and placed himself beside him, his expression similar to Esteban's. Doña Elvira said, her eyes fixed fondly upon her grandson:

'When Pedrillo was born his hair was lint-white, and his eyes never changed from blue. Perhaps as he grows older he will become darker and more like his father.' She longed for a clutch of grandchildren, and wished Luis would hurry up and get married.

'That is very probable,' Laurel agreed to please her, and Luis added:

'Fair Spaniards are not so rare. Our Castilian ancestor had golden hair. The child may be a throwback to him.'

Laurel sighed, wishing she knew her origins

and could trace her family back so far. She would never know what hers had been. Her eyes went involuntarily to Luis, and found he was regarding her with the now familiar intent gaze. Naturally he would choose a wife with a pedigree a mile long, when he got round to looking for one, or had he made his selection already? The introduction of Joanna must have deeply wounded his family pride.

'You must not look so sad,' Esteban said softly. 'We are happy to have you here, and we are your friends.'

Over his shoulder, Laurel caught Mercedes' malignant gaze. That one was an enemy.

'Pedrillo must have a tutor,' Doña Elvira announced decidedly, 'to instruct him in his native tongue.'

'He's not yet five,' Laurel reminded her. 'Isn't that a little young for serious lessons? He'll pick up a lot from hearing it spoken.'

'The servants all speak Andaluz,' his grandmother objected. 'He must speak Castilian like a well bred *hidalgo*.'

'Which he will never be, with his parentage,' Mercedes said nastily.

'Mercedes, for shame!' Luis expostulated, adding emphatically: 'He *is* your nephew.'

Mercedes gave him a severe look, compressing her lips.

Peter looked at her wonderingly, and declared with childish candour: 'That lady doesn't like me, and I don't like her.'

Mercedes stood up, smoothing her plain skirt.

'I will not stay to be insulted by that woman's brat! She brought Pedro nothing but shame and humiliation—and so will he if you keep him!'

She swept out of the room, and a general sigh of relief went up at her exit.

'Mercedes grows more sour every day,' Esteban remarked. 'We will all be a deal happier when she enters her convent.'

'Be more understanding, my son,' his mother chided him. She turned to Laurel apologetically. 'My daughter had a disappointment in her youth, poor girl, and it has embittered her. Now she has decided to devote herself to God.'

'I'm sorry,' Laurel murmured, not knowing what else to say. Other girls had disappointments, as the Señora put it, but they didn't become spiteful and venomous. It was to be hoped the nuns would imbue Mercedes with Christian charity, which seemed to be woefully lacking, and she would be out of the house before Peter came to live there.

To change the subject, Luis told them:

'I want to take Laurel and the boy up to Ronda. The new hotel there was Pedro's patrimony and will become his. He should see his heritage.'

Doña Elvira sighed. 'Your grandfather was cousin to a *marqués*, and you have become a tradesman!'

Luis laughed goodhumouredly. 'A much more profitable thing to be than an obsolete nobleman—you must move with the times, Mama.'

Peter, who had just taken in what he had said, was staring at him round-eyed.

'A hotel . . . all mine?' he gasped.

'Every stone in it, when you come of age.'

Laurel too was taken aback. Luis had told her he owned several hotels, but she had no idea that Peter could claim one of them. She caught his quizzical glance and knew he guessed her thoughts—uncanny how he was able to read them.

'Worth coming to Spain for?' he asked in a low voice.

'For Peter, yes,' for she would get nothing out of it except to lose the boy. 'Where is this place?'

'Ronda? It is a very old town up in the mountains, and is distinguished by being split in two by a nine-hundred-feet deep gorge. You will find it fascinating.'

'I'm sure I shall,' but she was wondering if she dared spend a day alone with Luis, for Peter hardly counted. Esteban too seemed to have a similar idea, though for a different reason, for he said:

'Mind if I come along too? Señorita Laurel is too young and pretty to risk her reputation without a *dueña*.'

'She is family,' Luis said curtly.

'But not within the table of affinity. You know what a nasty tongue Mercedes has, and she did not fancy our guest. Besides, I would like to see Ronda again myself. I have not been there since the *corrida* last December.' He turned to Laurel.

'Though it was the home of Pedro Romero, our most famous torero, it only has one *fiesta* a year.' His eyes kindled. 'He introduced fighting on foot, face to face with the bull. Before that it was always done on horseback, and he was reputed to have killed six thousand bulls without having been gored once.'

Laurel shuddered. 'Horrible!'

'What not getting gored? Oh, *claro*!' He looked dashed. 'You are English and side with the bull, though quite a lot of your countrymen watch the *corridas*.'

'I don't know how they can,' Laurel murmured, looking at Luis, and caught his faintly scornful smile.

She must never forget he was Spanish, and his race was capable of great cruelty. The Inquisition had been a Spanish institution. If she allowed herself to become emotionally involved with him she could expect no mercy. He would use her and throw her away without compunction. At least Pedro had married Joanna, whatever he had done to her afterwards, but Pedro had been a good deal younger than Luis, who would never commit such a folly for the sake of love. As it was, he was thinking she was feeble and squeamish to be revolted by the bloody spectacle which he no doubt enjoyed. She must find an excuse not to go to Ronda with him.

But all her wise resolutions vanished like dew before the sun when she found herself alone with him that same evening. After a comparatively early dinner by Spanish standards at eight o'clock, the tired child dropped off at once into exhausted sleep, and one of the maids told her she had been instructed to keep an eye on him if the Señorita wished to patronise the bar for a drink and to find company. Laurel did not wish for either, but she was too restless to stay in her room. She wandered out on to the terrace on to which the bar opened. The nights were still chilly, and the patrons preferred its shelter to the fresh air outside. So the terrace was deserted. It faced towards the sea, and the myriad lights of Fuengirola spread a carpet of stars along the border of the ocean. She was leaning over the balustrade gazing at them, when Luis came noiselessly to join her. Her heart gave a hard throb when she caught sight of him. He had dined with his mother and his evening clothes made him look every inch a Spanish grandee. She said uncertainly:

'I'm glad to see you, I want to talk to you.' For it was not good for Peter to dine at night in the hotel restaurant.

'I am enchanted to hear you say so.'

She was irritated by his exaggerated speech. 'It's only about Peter. Is he to go on living here?'

'Why not? Are you not comfortable? Just relax and enjoy yourself while he becomes used to us all.'

'Late dinner in the evening is not suitable for a young child.'

'Not according to English ideas.' Was there a faint sneer in his voice? In every nerve she was conscious of his tall figure looming over her. 'What arrangement would you suggest?'

'I don't want to upset the staff . . .'

'They are here to serve you. I assume a light supper served in one of the lounges would meet the case, then you can have your own meal later on in peace.'

Involuntarily she murmured, 'Alone.'

'Whose company would you like?' He moved a little nearer. 'Mine?'

'Oh, I expect I'll soon make some friends,' she said quickly, edging away from him. If only he wasn't so disturbing!

'You would find it distasteful?'

'Of course I didn't mean that,' she said crossly. 'But you're the big noise around here and it would make me conspicuous.'

He laughed, a low, sexy sound that stirred her blood.

'You are very discreet, Laurel, but you could join me in my suite.'

'That would be very indiscreet.'

'But very enjoyable.' He began to stroke her arm from which the full sleeve had fallen back, and his touch set her blood on fire. Someone in the bar-lounge was playing a guitar, and a little breeze moaned in the palm trees below them. Eroticism breathed in the scented air, and Laurel flung back her head, striving to free herself from its spell. It came in contact with his shoulder and he buried his face in the soft waves of her hair, while his arm crept round her waist.

'You are very sweet, Laurel.' His voice came muffled.

Making a supreme effort, she wrenched herself away from him.

'Are you trying to seduce me?' she asked desperately. 'In the circumstances isn't that in rather bad taste?'

Again he laughed softly. 'Are you seduceable?'

'No,' she cried vehemently. 'Oh, please, Luis, this isn't what I'm here for.'

He drew back and said in a completely changed voice,

'I apologise. I see I have misjudged you. The little episode this afternoon misled me.'

When she had responded to his kisses; she blushed in the darkness at the recollection. 'I . . . I don't know what came over me. I must have been crazy.'

'Delightful craziness.' She sensed he was smiling. 'But dangerous if you do not want to follow it through. I came to ask you to come up to my rooms.' She stiffened. 'I do all my business there, and I want more information about Peter.'

'Can't we talk here?'

'It is becoming cold. I have no evil intentions towards you, Laurel, you can trust me now that I know where I stand. I do not make the same mistake twice.'

This speech which should have been reassuring, Laurel found singularly unsatisfactory, but what *did* she want from him? He had evidently believed she was available, and finding she was not, had withdrawn. The wild rapture she had felt in his arms had not been shared, his emotion being much more commonplace, and he had put the wrong interpretation upon her response. Now she had put him right, he had become the stately Spanish Don again and she need have no qualms. Feeling chagrined, she said brightly:

'I'm ready, if you'll show me the way.'

Luis' suite, bedroom, sitting room and bathroom on the second floor, was plainly but expensively furnished. There was a large desk in one corner of the sitting room, evidence that he did do his business there, but before the window, which opened on to the balcony, there were tapestry-covered chairs, a small settee, and a coffee table. There was no *reja* to impede the view, which was over the swimming pool to rising ground opposite which culminated in a rocky prominence, once part of a castle's fortifications, which now housed a shrine.

Luis settled Laurel on the couch with a cushion behind her back, and went to pour her a glass of sherry.

'You said you were never told how Joanna got herself out of Spain without a passport,' he asked, watching the amber liquid fill the glass. 'Did you ever wonder?'

'I wondered about lots of things,' she admitted, 'but if I pressed Jo for confidences she became hysterical. From something she let drop, I imagine she was smuggled across in a private yacht.'

He nodded. 'I suspected that. Most of her unscrupulous friends down on the coast owned ocean-going craft. Those friends were one of the things she and Pedro quarrelled about.'

He brought her the sherry, setting it down upon the table. Laurel sipped it, then seeking to defend her sister, said:

'But if he was busy all day, she must have been very lonely by herself in that villa. Apparently *his* friends weren't exactly matey.'

Stiff-necked Spaniards, who kept to themselves, Joanna had told her.

'There are plenty of pleasant English people living in the locality, but they are unable to rise to yachts and diamond necklaces.'

'But didn't Pedro give her the necklace?'

Luis was studying the wine in his glass. 'Presumably,' he said evasively. Laurel looked at him suspiciously, but his face was expressionless.

'I don't know what you're implying,' she said slowly. 'But I won't listen to any nasty insinuations about poor Jo. I . . . I loved my sister.' She choked. Then to her horror tears started to her eyes and ran down her cheeks, for she had not yet recovered from the agony of loss Joanna's death had caused her. They had been very close before her marriage, two alone against the bewildering world of authority that had ruled their childhood. She fumbled for her handkerchief and became aware that Luis was beside her, his arm about her shoulders, as he pushed a large white one into her hands.

'*Querida*, please, please not to weep,' he besought her distractedly. Could this be Luis' voice, that hard, sophisticated man with that tender note in it? She turned her face into his chest, as he held her closer. '*Pequeña*, it is all over now. You must never go back to that dreary life. You shall have Pedro's villa, and I . . . we will take care of you.'

What heaven that would be, she thought, always to have his strength to support her, and wept harder, because of course it was impossible. Men didn't make such offers without expecting a return, and she couldn't pay his price.

'Please dry your tears,' he bade her softly. 'You are soaking my shirt.'

She raised her head, smiling wanly, and wiped her eyes; the handkerchief smelt of sandalwood. The liquid notes of the guitar came up to them from the lounge below, and now a man was singing, his deep voice full of passionate yearning. A bowl of lilies and jasmine on the desk gave out a heady perfume; Laurel lay against him, wrapped in a sensuous dream.

But the serpent was invading Eden. Luis moved uncomfortably, his nostrils flared slightly, and his breathing quickened, while tremors ran through Laurel's limbs. Gently she withdrew herself from his clasp, and he stood up. Going to the window, he closed it, and the song faded on a dying note. He came back and finished the wine in his glass, and when she was sure of her voice, she told him quietly:

'You're very generous, Luis, and oh, how I

wish I could stay, but it isn't possible.'

'Why not?'

Was he being deliberately obtuse? He must know he was a match to her tinder; already she was longing to be back in his arms, to feel his lips on hers. Or did he know it very well and wanted to cash in upon the physical attraction between them? What would his family think of such an arrangement, and the so suitable *señorita* he must marry? The very worst, even if it weren't true, and she didn't want to be present when Luis was courting his intended bride. She said steadily:

'Because I'm English, and I don't want to live permanently in Spain. I'm independent and don't want to be beholden to anybody. I would like to marry, and probably shall, but it must be to an Englishman—we've seen how disastrous a mixed marriage can be, and I'm unlikely to meet an eligible husband here.'

Luis' eyes narrowed. 'You already have one in mind?'

She smiled. 'A possibility,' she lied.

He gave her a long smouldering look, and she tried to meet it bravely.

'*Bueno*, you sound very positive, but you have only been here a few hours.' (It seemed more like a year.) 'I hope you will change your mind and learn to love Andalucia so much you will not want to leave it.'

But it wasn't Andalucia she was learning to love.

CHAPTER FOUR

LAUREL was awakened next morning by Peter thumping her pillow and pulling her hair.

'Wake up, wake up! It's time to go swimming.'

She rubbed the sleep out of her eyes. 'Good heavens, child, I've got to bathe and dress . . .'

'Not if you're going in the pool.'

She remembered Luis' threat to include her in the swimming lessons; she would like to acquire a little more suntan before exposing herself in a swimsuit; white limbs looked so naked among the bronzed bodies.

'It's too early,' she said firmly, looking at her watch. 'They won't have uncovered the pool yet,' for a net was drawn over it at night, 'and we must have breakfast.'

It was only half past seven.

Peter looked mutinous. 'Can I go and 'mind Tio Luis?' he suggested. ''Case he's forgotten?'

Luis would not appreciate the intrusion of this small imp at that hour, though he was probably up to take advantage of the morning cool, as most Spaniards did, taking a siesta during the hot afternoons, but, Laurel thought mischievously, he had better learn to cope with small boys against the time when he had one of his own.

'Very well,' she agreed, and told him the room number.

She took a leisurely bath, wondering if Peter would return crestfallen, but he didn't. Full marks for Uncle Luis! Dressed in her white outfit, she sat down to attend to her face, her mind reverting to the previous evening.

Before she left him, Luis had presented her with a thick wad of peseta notes, saying vaguely, 'For current expenses.' When she had protested he had told her not to be silly. She was giving up her time for Peter's benefit and at least she must have pocket money if not a salary, and she must come to him when she needed more.

Laurel had finally accepted the money, though with reluctance. Doña Elvira had sent to them their tickets to Malaga, but her resources were perilously low, as Luis had surmised, which was thoughtful of him, though it irked her pride. She had said hastily that she was sure it would be ample for her small needs.

He had given her another of his penetrating looks, and told her caustically she should make the most of her opportunities, to which she had retorted that although the amount might be chickenfeed to him, she was not a sponger, a statement that seemed to amuse him.

They had parted with the usual handshake, though she had half expected him to kiss her, and was furious with herself for the keen disappointment she felt at this omission. Kisses must be strictly forbidden if she were to retain her sanity.

She had told Luis the truth when she had said she hoped to marry; it was the only way she could ever have a family of her own, and though no likely candidate for matrimony had yet presented himself, she was only twenty-four, and there was plenty of time. During the last three years she had had little opportunity to go out with men friends and had had to turn down those who had asked her, but now she would be on her own, and she could probably hitch up with one she liked— but, she thought ruefully, it was not going to be easy to eliminate the memory of jet black eyes in an aquiline brown face.

Laurel had not hurried, for Peter was presumably with his uncle and she did not want to join in the swimming session. She was thinking she ought to go in search of him when the boy came in carrying a dripping pair of underpants, and two thousand-peseta notes, which he plonked down on the table in front of her.

'Tio says you must buy me some swimming trunks and those wing things to put on my arms,' he told her. 'Then I can go in alone as he won't always be here. We can get them in Mijas.'

They looked at each other doubtfully.

'I'd much rather he was around,' Peter added dolefully.

'So would I,' Laurel agreed—for Peter's sake, of course. 'But we mustn't forget he's a busy man. We'll go shopping after breakfast, if your grandmother doesn't send for you.'

Peter didn't look very enthusiastic about that,

though he brightened when he remembered Pom-pom. He was passionately devoted to animals, and the restrictions of the flat had prevented him from keeping a pet. Laurel thought that if he could be given a puppy it might help to console him when she had to leave him.

But when they came into reception, they were informed that Señora de las Aguilas sent her compliments, but regretted she could not receive them that day as she had one of her migraines.

Feeling they had been granted a holiday, Laurel and Peter ran down the wide marble stairs lined with the universal aspidistras to the buffet where breakfast was served, for although the Hotel Isabella was only three storeys high from ground level, owing to the steep incline of the hill a large portion of it was below it, and here the buffet and restaurant were situated. The large central table was heaped with many varieties of bread rolls, conserves, fruit juices, fresh fruit, and there were hardboiled eggs for those who fancied them. On a counter coffee and tea were available in glass jugs on hotplates.

Peter was charmed and helped himself lavishly. They sat down at a table by the floor-to-ceiling glass windows along the outer wall. These looked on to a paved terrace, a grass lawn and an ancient olive tree. In very hot weather they were slid open, so the guests could sit outside. The manager himself came to speak to them and ensure that they all had what they wanted, being anxious to please his boss. Of Luis there was no sign.

Breakfast over, they set out to explore the town.

Mijas was built along a shelf in the mountains, steep tree-clad slopes going up behind it terminating in craggy peaks. They came first to an open square, below the rocky eminence Laurel had seen from Luis' window, which had once been a fortress. The streets were on several levels, connected by steep picturesque alleyways. Mijas' most advertised feature was the donkeys, *burro-taxis* they were called, provided to assist visitors up the slopes. A group of these patient little beasts were gathered in the square waiting for hire. Peter clamoured for a ride, but Laurel could not bring herself to mount one, they looked too small to bear an adult's weight, though other people had no qualms. While he was gone she wandered among the nearer souvenir shops, which sold enormous Mexican hats, Spanish shawls, flamenco dolls, leather goods, inlaid woodwork which was done on the premises and every sort of bric-à-brac. She bought a miniature matador's sword, which she knew Peter would love, as well as the trunks and water-wings, the two latter articles going in her capacious white handbag.

It was as Peter descended from his long-eared mount that she caught sight of Luis coming across the square towards them. Unlike the tourists, he wore a cream linen jacket, for the upper-class Spaniard is still formal in his dress, with a panama hat tilted at a rakish angle. Laurel's heart began to perform acrobatics as he approached, but Peter saved her the necessity of speaking, as he called shrilly:

'Hi, Tio Luis, I've learned to ride!'

Luis glanced contemptuously at the donkey.

'A poor mount for a *caballero*. We must get you a pony.'

'A pony?' Peter gazed at him ecstatically. 'Ooh, a pony! And a dog, and a cat . . .'

'No, not a menagerie,' his uncle said firmly. He turned to Laurel. 'What do you think of Mijas?'

'I haven't seen much of it yet,' she told him, now in complete control of herself. 'I've just bought Peter's things . . .'

'What's that?' Peter interrupted, catching sight of the sword, which would not go in her bag.

'A little present for you.'

'Trash,' Luis muttered, but he smiled indulgently at the boy's delight in the toy. 'When you have finished waving that lethal weapon about, let me show you the bullring where it is used.'

'Is there one?' Laurel asked doubtfully.

He gave her a satirical grin. 'Of course, but there is also a fine view from the top of the hill where it is situated.'

'That will be more to my liking.'

He conducted them up a steep slope at the side of the castle rocks, and they came out on the top in an open space, on which there was a church, a magnificent view as promised, for the ground dropped sheer away on the farther side to the rolling country below, and the bullring. It was not very large and used only very occasionally, but weather-worn posters were evidence that it was. Luis showed Peter the entrance through which the bull came, which he must call *toro*.

'*Toro, burro*—soon I know lots of words,' the boy declared proudly.

'The sooner the better,' Luis observed drily.

They went into the small circular arena, and Peter became wildly excited, rushing about shouting: 'Come on, *toro*, come and fight me, *toro*!' waving his sword, until his uncle captured him.

'Calm down, *chico*! You appear to have the Spanish excitable temperament, and their delight in making a noise.' He said it with satisfaction. 'Shall we go back and find some refreshment?'

They returned the way they had come, and found an open-air café, wedged in a corner, a few steps up from the road. Luis seated them at a table under a striped umbrella and a waiter came hurrying to take their order. Laurel looked about her with pleasure, at the white buildings on either side, the stairway behind them going up to a higher level, with above them the blue sky, and in front a border of roses between them and the street. The sun poured down, the golden sunshine which brought so many people to Spain.

'This is nice,' she said contentedly.

'Ah, Andalucia is beginning to weave its spell about you.'

She met his laughing glance across the table, and there was a wicked glint in his black eyes. His brown, shapely hand lay within inches of her own on the table top, and she dropped her eyes to it, aware of turmoil in her breast. It was not his country that had laid a spell on her, but the man himself, a dark enchantment that chained her senses. He covered her slender fingers with his own. 'Cannot you bear to look at me?' he asked softly.

Every nerve thrilled at his touch. Far from decreasing, his fascination grew with each passing moment. Peter was gazing up at a caged canary hanging on the houses opposite, pouring out its little heart in song, and did not notice their clasped hands.

'The sun is in my eyes,' Laurel explained. 'I must put on my dark glasses.' She made to withdraw her hand, but Luis' grip tightened.

'Then I shall not be able to watch your expressions. You have very eloquent eyes, Laurel, they show your moods.'

Which was exactly why she wanted to obscure them. She gave him a nervous smile, and then to her relief the waiter arrived with their refreshment, ice cream for Peter, orange juice for her and beer for Luis.

As soon as her hand was free, and he loosed it as soon as the man approached, Laurel fished out her sunglasses from her handbag and fixed them firmly on her nose.

'Eclipsed,' she said provocatively.

'If we were not in a public place, I would soon have them off, and perhaps . . .' his eyes went to the narrow bands supporting the top of her sleeveless cotton blouse, 'other things besides.'

It was the first time he had made a suggestive remark, and Laurel looked at him disdainfully.

'I think you must have got a touch of the sun,' she rebuked him.

His face changed, became sombre, and he sat back in his chair, seeming to withdraw into himself.

'You are an enticing little witch, Laurel,' he said coldly, 'but you do right to remind me that I cannot affort to indulge in midsummer madness.'

'Who's mad?' Peter enquired, his interest caught.

'Your uncle has occasional bouts of lunacy,' Luis informed him. 'Fortunately they can be controlled before any real damage is done.' He turned his shoulder to Laurel, as he informed the boy that on the morrow he had to go on business to Seville, but the day after they would go to Ronda.

'To see my hotel?'

'And other things.' He began to talk about that town, but his manner was abstracted. Laurel felt she had been snubbed by this exclusion, but what else could she expect? To flirt with Luis was to play with fire, and they both knew it. It would have been more generous to allow her to be the one to withdraw, but perhaps he feared she wouldn't. It was galling to think that he might imagine she wanted to encourage him.

Their refreshments finished, he asked when Peter was going to see his grandmother, almost as if he suspected she was trying to keep him from her, which was totally unjust. Coldly she explained about the migraine, of which it seemed he had not been informed, adding that in the meantime she supposed they could amuse themselves as they pleased.

'Riding *burros*?' he asked with a sneer. 'You are not *turistas*.'

'We are this morning,' she retorted. 'Don't be stuffy, Luis—all this,' with a sweep of her hand she indicated the crowded square, 'is new and exciting to us both.'

'You are easily pleased.' Then he begged to be excused—he had an errand to perform, and must leave them. 'Do not stay too long out in the sun,' were his parting words.

'Why does he change like that?' Peter, who was a perceptive child, demanded. 'First he was quite matey, then he goes all snooty.'

'He must have remembered some business worry,' Laurel said vaguely. Luis had changed because he had recalled his position and that it hardly became it to be exchanging backchat with a little nobody in public, for in spite of his gallantries, that was all she was to him.

Next morning, Peter refused to go in the pool in spite of the water-wings, and loudly deplored his uncle's absence. Laurel was still trying to persuade him when Esteban came out of the hotel to tell her his mother had recovered and wanted him to fetch Pedrillo to spend the morning with her and stay to lunch. He seemed embarrassed, and guessing what was troubling him, Laurel declared it was an excellent idea to have Pedro to herself for a while. He seemed relieved and flashed her a grateful smile.

'*Bueno*, she thinks he will more quickly adjust if you are not always with him. Not that we do not appreciate your care of him, *comprende*?'

She did, all too well. Grandmother wanted to wean Peter from her as quickly as possible. He went off quite happily with Esteban, 'to see Pompom.' The dog was much more to his fancy than the lady.

The hotel seemed extraordinarily empty without Luis and Peter, though there were plenty of pleasant people willing to talk to her. Laurel had her hair done—the place had its own beauty salon—and lay in the sun, treating her arms and legs with sun lotion. She was pleased to see they were browning nicely. Esteban brought Peter back at siesta time, and was quite prepared to flirt with her, but Laurel was not responsive, for Peter seemed subdued and she knew there was something wrong. She said the boy needed a nap and she must take him indoors, much to Esteban's disgust.

'*Hasta mañana*,' he said, shaking her hand and gazing soulfully into her eyes. 'I am hoping his business keeps Luis in Sevilla, and we can go without him. He . . . what do you say, cramps my style.'

Thank God for that, Laurel thought, for she had no wish to become involved with the young Spaniard, though he was nearer her own age than his brother. Although she knew Luis' society was far from good for her, she was looking forward to the expedition . . . in his company.

Their room was dim and cool, the chambermaid having drawn the curtains against the sun; not being sun-starved like the British, the natives knew the value of shade.

'Well, darling, how did it go?' Laurel asked cheerfully.

'Oh, fine, Tia. I played with Pom-pom and she gave me lots of sweets. I had fish for my dinner and strawberries and cream.'

She took off his shoes, and he lay down on the bed.

'Tia?'

'Yes, darling?' She sat down beside him on the bed.

'All my toys and things have come, she showed me a little room where they are, and lots of new ones too, it's to be my room and . . . and I'm to sleep there soon.'

Laurel was angry. Peter had had too many upsets lately, he should be given time to adjust himself before making further changes. Doña Elvira was going too fast.

'It will be nice to have your own room,' she said carefully.

'But . . . but there wasn't one for you.' His voice rose to a wail. 'Where will you be? I want to be with you!'

'I expect your granny hasn't got another spare room,' Laurel said soothingly, stroking his hair, wondering if this were true. 'I'll be here, just across the yard. I can probably see your room from my window. You're growing into a big boy, darling, and old enough to have your own room. You can't always sleep in mine.'

'That's what Granny said, but you won't ever go away?'

She repeated what she had said before, 'Not while you need me,' and wondered for how long that would be. One thing was certain, she could not leave yet, however much caution warned her; she should not stay near Luis.

'That will be always,' Peter said drowsily. He fell asleep holding her hand. Laurel sat watching his sleeping face. She had no place here in this foreign land, and eventually she would have to move on. Her employers had promised they would keep her place for her if she returned within a reasonable time, but it was monotonous work. She was rootless, homeless, with only this small scrap of humanity belonging to her, and him she must relinquish for his own good. Could she possibly find employment in Andalucia so they would not be completely sundered? Luis had wanted her to make her home there, but his offer of the villa must have been during one of his 'bouts of lunacy', of which he had spoken on the previous morning, and then withdrawn. He knew very well they were safer apart. There was no niche for her in the Aguilas hierarchy, and Peter would grow away from her as time passed. Better to make a clean break and make a new life for herself, however dreary the prospect.

As Luis had arranged, Peter was served an early supper, after which he played in the garden for a while, and was in bed and asleep when Laurel went to the restaurant for her own meal. A young couple at her table had seen her with Peter and not unnaturally thought he was her own child, and she didn't think they believed her when she said he was her nephew, but she had no wish to explain her connection with the Aguilas and their rather strange arrangements. Afterwards, crossing the foyer, Esteban came breezing in and waylaid her.

'Come and have a drink with me in the lounge.'

'I was going to Peter . . .'

'Oh, Carmen will keep an ear open for him.' He turned to the desk and spoke to one of the female clerks. She nodded and smiled coquettishly. '*Si, si, señor.*'

He swept Laurel through the door into the bar-lounge. She raised no further objection; he would enliven a lonely evening. She asked for coffee, but he insisted she have a cognac with it. When they had been served, he leaned back in the luxurious armchair—the lounge was furnished with very comfortable ones—lit a cigarette, after offering her one, which she refused, and surveyed her through the rising smoke.

'You are very lovely, Laurel. If your sister was like you, I never saw her. I was doing my military service while she was here, I am not surprised that Pedro lost his head over her.'

'Beauty can pall if other things aren't right,'

Laurel said drily, 'and I think you're a flatterer, Esteban. What time will your brother be back?'

She had a suspicion that Luis would not be pleased to find her tête-à-tête with Esteban, though she could see no harm in it.

'In the small hours. He will be dining with the Ordoñez, who live in Sevilla. Pedro was to have married Cristina Ordoñez, but since he jilted her, Luis is considering marrying her himself.'

'I should think the lady would fight shy of another Aguilas,' Laurel observed, aware of a sudden chill.

'*Querida*, women do not fight shy of Luis, as you put it, they fall over themselves to win his favours.'

Laurel did not recognise the endearment, and was too perturbed by what Esteban had told her to resent it if she had. But why should she mind? Luis had told her he was expected to marry, and no doubt this girl was entirely suitable to be his wife, if she had been selected for Pedro. She took a sip of her cognac and found it steadying.

'What's she like, this Señorita Ordoñez?' she asked with assumed casualness.

'Dark, handsome—Luis would never contemplate marrying a plain woman. Very rich, of course, and inclined to be jealous as most Spanish women are.' He laughed merrily. 'I bet Luis will keep quiet about taking you and the brat up to Ronda tomorrow.'

'She has no cause to object to that,' Laurel said with dignity. 'I'm not a competitor.'

'No? Do not forget a girl with your complexion robbed her of her first suitor.'

'For that reason, Luis avoids me.'

'I have seen no evidence of that,' Esteban laughed again. 'Didn't he follow you up into the town yesterday?'

'He had an errand there.'

'Did you believe that? You are being naïve, Laurel—you know you are damned attractive.' The drink was loosening his tongue. 'If I were Cristina I would insist you return to England on the next plane.'

'I don't suppose she knows I exist . . .'

'You underestimate the local grapevine. Everyone on the Costa del Sol will know of your arrival by now, and that you are a siren.'

Laurel half rose. 'I find this conversation distasteful . . .'

Esteban pushed her back into her seat. 'Please, do not desert me,' he besought her plaintively. 'We can find a more congenial one.'

'Congenial what?'

Both started violently as looking round, they saw Luis had come up to their table. He stood looming over them, and Laurel was overcome though she had no reason to feel guilty. Esteban smiled up at his brother sunnily.

'*Que tal*, Luis, I thought you were still in Sevilla. I was trying to console Laurel for your absence, and . . .' a malicious sparkle came into his eyes, 'explaining your involvement with

Cristina, about which you had neglected to inform her.'

'Why should I? And I have no involvement with Señorita Ordoñez ... yet,' Luis returned coolly. 'You are an impudent puppy, Esteban.' His sombre gaze was fixed upon Laurel, who was busying herself with her coffee cup, and looking anywhere but at him. 'Now suppose you take yourself back to Mama, who, I am sure, does not know you are here.'

'*Nombre de Dios!*' The young man sprang to his feet, pouring forth a flood of vehement Spanish, which caused the other occupants of the lounge to stare at them curiously. Luis cut him short with a few curt words, and after bowing to Laurel with a muttered, '*Buenas noches,*' Esteban strode out of the lounge.

Luis sank down in his vacated chair, and beckoned to a waiter. He ordered a brandy and soda, then turned to Laurel apologetically.

'Please forgive his bad manners.'

'You provoked him,' she retorted. 'He's still young and sensitive, and you spoke to him as if he were a delinquent teenager.'

'So you rush to defend him. How come you were here together anyway?' His black eyes were smouldering.

'Why shouldn't we be? He offered me a drink and I was feeling lonely. Am I supposed to be in purdah?'

'I would like to put you there,' he said savagely. 'It is where women like you should be kept. Has it not occurred to you that your precious sister caused enough disruption in our family without you following in her footsteps?'

The arrival of the waiter with his drink checked the furious words that rose to her lips. When he had gone, she said icily:

'I shall treat that remark with the contempt it deserves. Now I'm going to bed. Goodnight, *señor*.'

She would have risen, but leaning forward, he shot out his hand and grasped her wrist with a grip of steel. 'Stay where you are!'

His touch sent fire coursing through her veins. She sank back murmuring, 'You're hurting me.'

'Then do as you are told.' He released her wrist, and took a swig of his drink. 'Esteban is, as you say, young and also impressionable. I would be obliged if you do not try to corrupt him.'

'That's an insulting thing to say! I've no designs upon your brother whatever.'

A smile flickered over his face. 'But he may have on you.'

'Then I'm afraid he'll be disappointed.'

Luis gave a long sigh, drained his glass and wiped his mouth with the paper serviette provided.

'*Ay mi*, Laurel, have you any idea what that pale beauty of yours does to the men of the South?'

Laurel felt a little thrill of gratification. He really did think she was beautiful and the men of the South would include himself, but she answered sedately:

'I can't help my looks, and I don't see that having a drink with Peter's uncle constitutes such a heinous offence. Don't you want us to be friends?'

'I distrust friendship between men and women.' He looked away across the crowded lounge with unseeing eyes. 'I meant to visit the Ordoñez tonight to make a formal offer for Cristina's hand.'

Laurel's heart seemed to stop. 'Why didn't you?' she asked quietly.

'She had gone to Madrid.' He turned his head and their eyes met. She saw a red gleam in the dark depths of his and her own fell to the table top.

'But she'll come back?'

'*Si*, I am afraid she will.'

'Luis, you aren't suffering from another bout of lunacy?' she asked sweetly.

'Provoking witch,' he growled. 'Oh, go to bed, Laurel, this conversation is unprofitable.' His voice dropped to a whisper: 'I only wish I could come with you.'

Desire, hot and palpitating was there between them, desire that could not, must not be assuaged. Laurel got to her feet and found she was trembling. With an effort she controlled herself.

'Do we still go to Ronda tomorrow?' she asked, and was surprised her voice sounded so normal.

'But of course.' A flash of white teeth in his dark face. 'Esteban and I will chaperon each other.' He stood up. '*Buenas noches*, Laurel, sleep well.'

For a long moment they stared at each other, blue eyes meeting black, then with a sigh, Laurel turned away.

'Goodnight, Luis.'

Quietly she went out of the lounge.

CHAPTER FIVE

THE way to Ronda from Mijas wound through
magnificent country, with gaunt piles of mountains rising from the undulating ground. The two
men sat in the front seats of the Silver Shadow,
with Laurel and Peter in the back. She had been
offered the passenger seat, but said she preferred
to be with the child. Luis had given her a quizzical
look, but made no comment, but Esteban had
grinned and remarked:

'The lady is very discreet.'

'She needs to be, with you around,' Luis
retorted, which she took to be a veiled allusion to
the night before. If Esteban had been driving, she
might have taken the offered place, for she
thought his feelings had been hurt by his brother's
caustic dismissal, but she wanted to avoid intimacy with Luis—no, 'wanted' was the wrong
word—but she knew it was unwise. She was
wearing her beige trousers, with a white blouse,
and a long sleeveless over-jacket which came
nearly to her knees, a concession to Spanish susceptibilities. It was in knitted acrylic, with a
metallic thread running through it, which toned
with her hair. Esteban had paid her a flowery
compliment when she had appeared in it, but Luis
had not even glanced at her. He was no doubt

regretting what he had told her in the lounge on the previous evening. She looked yearningly at the black head in front of her. He meant to offer for Cristina when she returned from Madrid, and his fancy for herself would die a natural death. She could only hope her own infatuation would fade as quickly, but it showed no sign of abating, rather it increased every time she saw him. It was a little like sitting on a keg of gunpowder, she mused, any unexpected crisis could cause it to explode.

The predominant crop in that part of Spain is olives. There are acres and acres of the silvery-leaved trees, and they stretch up the mountains for as far as they can obtain a foothold. The upper portions of these precipitous peaks are bare rock and shale. There are other crops, including corn, but a great dearth of animals, except for goats, which browse along the verges and waste patches watched over by some ancient grandfather, gnarled by the sun. Luis explained that there was little pasture for cattle, especially farther north where the land was arid, few cows could be grazed and butter was considered a luxury. The peasants steeped their bread in oil.

Ronda proved to be, as he had promised, a fascinating city. Ringed by mountains, many feet above sea level, it was split by the Tajo, the sinister gorge caused by some earthquake in pre-historic times. It was spanned by three bridges, the New Bridge, a monumental piece of engineering, high above the deepest part of the gorge, and

two where it was much lower, opening to the
plain, an Arab one and a Roman. Houses clustered
along the edge of the Tajo, and Laurel thought
she would not like to live with such an abyss outside her back door. Having parked the car, they
walked across the New Bridge, gazing fearfully
into the depths on either side, and thence down a
narrow street beside it, to look up at it from
below. They were in the old part of the town, and
it was very old; Moor and Roman had left their
mark. Uphill again and past the summer palace of
the Marqués de Salvatierra, the façade of which
looked as though it could do with some redecorating.

'He should turn it into a hotel,' Luis said,
laughing. 'Then he could afford a lick of paint.'

Laurel knew he was thinking of his own well
kept residences. He might have stepped down
from the aristocracy, but he knew how to make
money, and had no regrets for loss of status. In
that respect, he was as modern in his outlook as
she was herself. They looked in at the Cathedral
of Santa Maria, but Peter's short legs were beginning to tire and he complained that he was
thirsty.

'We will lunch at the Hotel del Toro Negro,'
Luis decided. 'It is in the modern part of the
town, so we will go back to the car, if you can
walk that far, infant.' He slanted a mischievous
glance at Laurel. 'I do not think your aunt will
appreciate its decor, which consists of scenes from
the *corrida*.'

'Certainly I won't,' Laurel declared. 'Must we go there?'

'Yes, because it will be Pedrillo's inheritance.'

He did not only mean the hotel, but was reminding her that Peter was Spanish.'

'The frescos are famous,' Esteban told her, 'you must see them, they are so lifelike.'

'With all the gory details,' Luis murmured. He was regarding her with a lazy sensuous expression, a little cruel smile curling his handsome mouth.

'Peter will have nightmares,' she began, but he cut her short.

'No Aguilas was ever squeamish, and in due course he will enjoy a bullfight.'

'When can I see one?' Peter demanded.

'You'd hate it,' Laurel cried vehemently.

'Not he, he is a Spaniard.' Another reminder.

Laurel looked from one to the other of the dark, Latin faces of Peter's uncles, and they were probably right—Peter, for all his fairness, was of their kin. Suddenly she felt utterly alien, entirely alone. In silence she turned away and began to move down towards the bridge. She stumbled over a cobble, and her hand was taken and drawn through a strong arm.

'You are tired,' Luis said gently, 'we have walked you too far. Lean on me.'

'Peter . . .'

'Esteban is carrying him.'

Glancing behind her, she saw the child was sitting astride the young man's shoulders and clutching at his hair.

'Gee up, horsey!' he shouted gleefully.

To please him Esteban was tossing his head and making considerable detours.

'Oh, but I can't let Esteban . . .'

'Do him good,' Luis interrupted callously. 'Leave him less energy for . . . other things. Would you like that I carry you?'

'Thanks, no, I'm fine.'

But she was glad of his supporting arm. A moment ago she had been repelled by the realisation of the gulf between their points of view. Now his almost tender concern had drawn her close to him—literally. She could feel the hard muscles in his forearm through his thin sleeve. If only she could lean upon his strength for always, unload all her troubles and perplexities on to his broad back, become a meek, adoring Spanish wife . . . absurd fantasy! She was an independent British girl, and needed no masculine support. With an effort she returned to reality, and gently withdrew her arm.

'Thank you, I'm all right now, and it's not much farther.'

'Does contact with me repel you?'

What a question, when he must know very well how he could arouse her!

'You know it's not that, but . . . but . . .' She turned her head away, unable to explain.

'I understand.'

They had reached the bridge and they stopped to look down into the yawning chasm. A thread of water ran along its bottom.

'At this time of the year, the Guadalevin is a mere trickle,' Luis told her, 'but when it rains it becomes a raging torrent. Love between man and woman is like that, Laurel, one moment a placid stream and then, suddenly an overwhelming flood.'

'Only to subside again,' Laurel suggested in a strangled voice, for Pedro's and Joanna's passion had been exactly that, an irresistible spate, drying up into not even a trickle.

'What would you? If it maintained its full force it would eventually destroy the participants—that has been the end of most of the world's great love stories.' There spoke the cynic, the man of the world. 'Love should be enjoyed, Laurel, it should not be allowed to become a tragedy, and to make the most of it, it should be indulged when it reaches its peak before frustration sours it.' He began to stroke her bare arm. 'Laurel . . .' His voice was harsh with feeling.

'No!' she said sharply. She knew what he was going to say and she did not want to hear him say it. What was coming to life between them was to her beautiful, she did not want it to be tarnished, but he, being a man, thought only of consummation.

'I've never slept with a man,' she told him faintly, hot colour staining her cheeks.

Putting a hand on her shoulders, he turned her about to face him, staring intently into her eyes. She met his scrutiny bravely, seeing in the dark depths of his a flicker of flame.

'Is that true, Laurel?'

'Yes.' Unable to sustain that piercing gaze, her own eyes dropped, and she looked what she was, a shy young virgin.

'In that case . . .' he began slowly, but at that moment Esteban charged up beside them.

'Laurel, for pity's sake release me from this fiendish brat before he has pulled all my hair out by the roots!'

Luis hastily withdrew his hand—it seemed to her he was glad of the interruption. She said sharply, for the recoil of her own emotion was like the snap of an over-stretched elastic band.

'Put him down, Esteban, he can walk the rest of the way. It's your own fault, you should have come straight here.'

If he had she would not have made that foolish confession, now Luis would think she was immature or retarded; no doubt he preferred experienced women. But why should she mind? Did she want him to seduce her? She felt troubled and confused.

Esteban dropped a protesting Peter at her feet, and she went on: 'Don't make a fuss, Peter, you're too big to be carried—you can hold my hand.'

They crossed the bridge in silence, Laurel and a sulky Peter in front, the two men bringing up the rear.

The Toro Negro was palatial, in common with all the Aguilas properties, and as promised, the dining room walls were decorated with pictures of the different phases of the *corrida*. Peter was thrilled by them and poured out a volley of questions. Laurel could not check him, though as she had said, she foresaw nightmares when he went to bed.

The meal was excellent, and rather different from what was being served to the coachloads of tourists who occupied most of the room. They were placed at a secluded table, half hidden by a screen of iron tracery supporting a vine. There was crayfish and lobster for a starter, paella followed by roast lamb, and an iced pudding, covered with flaming chocolate, which had been specially prepared for the little master. The staff had been advised of their coming, and Peter was introduced to the manager, head waiter and the chef. *'Es un angelito!'* the last exclaimed, gazing enraptured at the boy's fair face.

Esteban stagemanaged the little ceremony, but Luis stood aloof. Looking towards him, Laurel caught a faint derisive smile on his lips and a satirical gleam in his eye. It occurred to her that he might not relish the thought of having to hand over the Toro Negro when the time came, which until Peter's advent he had come to regard as his own. With some idea of placating him, she said to him in a low voice:

'Peter may not want to be a hotelier when he grows up.'

'Naturally he must follow his bent,' Luis returned, 'which at the moment seems to incline towards the bullring.'

Laurel recoiled. 'Ah, never that!'

Luis laughed unkindly at her stricken look.

'Do not distress yourself. Men of good family do not become *toreros*.'

There was something in his voice and expression that she could not fathom, but she rarely had any clue to his thoughts, as he seemed so often to have to hers, and she felt unaccountably uneasy. Later, when they went out into the gardens, she forgot all about her unpleasant impression, but it was to recur to her at a future date.

The grounds were extensive, sloping downwards in terraces with paved paths and flights of steps, and a fine view over open country to the enclosing mountains. Masses of geraniums climbed over walls and spilled out of stone vases; palm trees waved their long fronds and there were clusters of roses everywhere—sweet-scented ones, not like the scentless modern varieties. There were clumps of huge agaves, a succulent that was common in that country, with long green and yellow leaves edged with spines, but these were going to flower, for tall buds on mastlike stems rose from the foliage. Peter was soon bored, and after giving them a quizzical look, Esteban took him off in search of something more amusing, but Luis and Laurel wandered on, not noticing their departure. Luis' manner towards her was gentle and protective; he extended a ready hand to assist her, whenever they came to a rough patch or steep steps. She did not resent it, this was an idyllic spot and she was lulled into contented euphoria, for he did not make any disturbing remarks, and for once, when he touched her, the spark did not ignite. For the most part they were silent, and the silence was one of perfect accord; they might have been strolling through Eden, the tall dark man, with the slender slip of a girl beside him.

Luis stopped by a bush of dark red roses, which exuded a strong perfume. He broke off one of the velvety blooms, touched it with his lips, and handed it to her.

'A memento of a lovely day,' he told her, his dark eyes as soft as the petals of the flower. 'A red rose of Ronda.'

Laurel pushed the stalk into the front of her blouse, her own eyes azure stars.

'I'll treasure it always.'

'*Ay mi*, it will fade, Laurel.'

'But not the memory.'

His face grew sombre, and he spoke with a touch of the melancholy that is part of the Spanish make-up and never far away.

'Memories also fade.'

But this one would remain vivid in hers. True, the rose would wither, but she would keep it always ... Oh, dear God, she was becoming as soppy and sentimental as any teenager—more so, for the modern teenager prides herself upon her sophistication. A Victorian miss would be a better comparison, didn't they press flowers in books to preserve them? As if he divined her thoughts in his uncanny way, Luis said softly:

'It is good to feel romantic occasionally in these hardboiled times.'

'Are you feeling romantic?' she asked wonderingly, because that seemed out of character.

'Who would not?' He smiled down at her. 'Red roses, a charming companion, the mood of the moment.'

The mood of the moment . . . it would pass.

He glanced at his watch. 'I am afraid it is time to go, we must find Peter and Esteban.'

'Oh dear!' Laurel had forgotten all about Peter. She quickened her steps towards the hotel. 'I shouldn't let Peter be such a bother to Esteban. Your brother is very goodnatured.'

'More so than I,' Luis observed drily.

'Oh, you have your good points,' Laurel said flippantly. With the reminder of the others, the charmed atmosphere was dissolving. He gave her a dark look.

'I am no chivalrous knight, Laurel, but a very human man.'

Was that a warning?

They found Peter and Esteban playing ball with an off-duty receptionist, who was flirting with Esteban. She vanished when she caught sight of Luis, and the young man gave them a worried look.

'We thought you had got lost.'

'So we were, for a little while, but we have returned to the mundane world, and it is time we left.' Luis threw Laurel a wry look. 'The sinners have been ejected from Paradise.'

'You do say funny things,' Peter told him. 'This isn't Para . . . Para . . . what you said, Tio Luis, that means Heaven, where Mummy is. This is just an ordinary garden.'

'So it is,' Laurel sighed.

But it had not seemed ordinary to her.

Luis laughed, and patted Peter on the head. 'Out of the mouths of babes . . .'

'I'm not a baby, Tio,' Peter protested, 'and you said you'd show me the bullring before we left.'

The harsher side of Spain.

Luis drove them back into the older part of the town. This Plaza de Toros was the largest in the world and the only one to have a stone parapet. An annual *corrida* was held there in honour of Pedro Romero, who had compiled the rules of modern bullfighting, and the Rondan style is considered the purest form of that sanguinary art. Luis showed Peter his statue before they left. The boy stared up at the proud arrogant face with awe.

'When I grow up I'm going to be a matador and kill six thousand bulls,' he declared.

His uncles laughed, but Laurel felt sick. The child didn't know what he was talking about, of course, nor did he connect the unfortunate bulls with his love of animals, but sometimes she wished he was not half Spanish, for lovable as he was, there might well be concealed in him the cruel streak she had detected in Luis.

'My name is Pedro too,' he added proudly, for the first time accepting the Latinised form of Peter.

Esteban suggested that they should return by the new road to Marbella and the coast; it was spectacular and Laurel would enjoy the run.

The road certainly was spectacular, running in long loops, blasted in places out of the living rock, with sheer mountain on one side and deep ravines on the other, but Laurel did not enjoy it. She gave a sigh of relief when they reached sea level and the coast, for though Luis was an excellent driver she had had qualms during the descent.

When she was back in the hotel, she put her rose in a glass of water. As she removed it from her blouse, a thorn pricked her bosom, the tiny drop of blood oozed up on her white skin, the same colour as the rose. Heart's blood, she thought wryly as she wiped it away, but if she were not wary, she might well receive a much deeper wound and one that could not be so easily staunched. For she knew now that she was falling in love with Luis, and could anything be more disastrous?

He desired her, she was not so naïve that she did not realise that, but desire was not love and he was going to marry the so suitable Señorita Cristina Ordoñez who lived in Seville. He would never dream of allying himself with Laurel Lester, dowerless and of unknown antecedents. Nor, with the fiasco of her sister's marriage, ever present in her mind, could she contemplate a union with a Spaniard. Pedro and Joanna had rushed into matrimony, and what a tragedy it had all been.

Luis had hinted at an affair, but that was out of

the question. Nameless orphan she might be, but she valued her integrity, and she was well aware that she was vulnerable. Although she was nearing her mid-twenties, she had never until now been strongly attracted to a man, and had felt no temptation to yield to the propositions which had been offered to her during her working life, the penalty for being good-looking and attractive. She had in fact been a little scornful of her colleagues' experiments, which seemed to have little to do with real or lasting love, and she had had no experience of the power of sex. What an irony of fate that two such incompatible beings should be drawn together by the chemical reaction of their bodies over which they had no control. But it must be controlled, because Peter's uncle was strictly forbidden. The Aguilas family had a poor enough opinion of the Lester girls without adding to it by embarking upon a liaison with its senior member, and she would hate to do anything to give Peter reason to be ashamed of her when he was old enough to understand.

Luis too must be well aware of all this, and in his heart knew there could never be anything between them. They had been given one idyllic day and that must content them. He would not want to risk his chances with Cristina by creating any gossip, and in a hotel like this one, scandal was quickly spread. He would realise, as she did only too well, that they must avoid each other in future. Eventually she would return to England and be severed from him for ever.

The fragrance of the rose filled the room, and she touched it gently with one fingertip. Red rose of Ronda—were not roses the epitome of romance? But her romance could only be, as Luis had said, the mood of a moment.

She would have her memories to look back upon in the lonely days ahead when Peter and Luis had forgotten her, and they must be her consolation. She felt tears start to her eyes as she contemplated the separation. Then Peter came bursting into the room demanding to know if his supper was ready, and she blinked them back as she went to minister to his needs.

The red rose dropped a petal on the wooden table where Laurel had placed it. It would not last long.

CHAPTER SIX

As the summer advanced, the weather became much hotter, the countryside took on a burnt-up look, the lawns surrounding the swimming pool had to be watered daily to keep them green. The days fell into a routine. In the early morning Peter swam, but with Esteban, not Luis. Then he went to the Casa for Spanish lessons, with a somewhat formidable middle-aged gentleman to whom surprisingly he took a fancy.

'He tells me lovely stories,' he confided to Laurel, 'all about El Cid, the Moors, Cortes and Piz . . . something, who conquered the Asticks and the Incas.'

'Aztecs,' Laurel corrected him mechanically. So Peter was also learning the history of his nation. He spent more and more time with his grandmother, who invited other children to play with him from impeccable Spanish families, but they never came to the hotel, occasionally he spent a night there—in his own room. Laurel knew her time there was running out.

She had little contact with Luis, she had hoped . . . and feared he would go away, for she gathered that he seldom stayed for long in one place, but he continued to live at the Reina Isabella and she was always conscious of his unseen presence.

Occasionally she encountered him in the foyer, the restaurant or on the terraces, and he would exchange a few polite commonplaces, but though their words were few, their eyes were eloquent, hers were unknowingly wistful, and his would kindle with smouldering fire. The attraction between them was undiminished, and their chance meetings were more of a torment than a pleasure. On the rare occasions when she was invited to the Casa, Doña Elvira referred to Cristina as Luis' *novia*, and the engagement seemed to be a foregone conclusion, except by the principals. Why, oh, why, Laurel thought despairingly, didn't Luis take himself off to Seville and clinch the matter? Esteban, who was more often at the Reina than his mother's house, told her that if his brother continued to procrastinate, the lady would become tired of waiting for him to declare himself and he would lose her. Mama was becoming anxious about it.

'Then what's he waiting for?' Laurel asked.

Esteban shrugged his shoulders, 'My brother is unpredictable,' and looked at her thoughtfully. But she couldn't be the impediment, for Luis would never turn from his duty because of her.

They were sitting by the pool, as Esteban had been giving her swimming lessons while Peter was absent. She was seeing a great deal of him, for he seemed to have taken it upon himself to entertain her. He was on holiday after completing his military service and was in no hurry to take up the management of yet another of the family hotels, which employment had been provided for him, declaring he deserved a long vacation after the rigours of army life.

'Mercedes blames you for his dilatoriness,' Esteban said bluntly.

'She would—your sister would like to blame me for everything,' Laurel declared a little bitterly, for the Spanish girl continued to be antagonistic in spite of all her endeavours to placate her; it seemed she could never forgive her for being Joanna's sister, 'but I'm not guilty. I've hardly exchanged more than a dozen words with Luis since we went to Ronda, and that's a fortnight ago.'

She sighed, recalling that perfect day, but Luis had made it very plain there was to be no aftermath, not that she had expected one, and he had left her swimming instruction to his brother.

She was reclining on one of the mattress-covered loungers, a towelling wrap more or less covering her one-piece swim suit, rather less than more. Their mattresses were set in the shade of the trees overhanging the garden, for it had become too hot to sit in the sun. She had tanned to a rich brown, against which her silvery hair made a striking contrast, and her eyes looked a brilliant hue. Esteban was gazing at her admiringly.

'Has Luis made love to you yet?' he asked suddenly.

Laurel sat up abruptly. 'Good God, no! What do you think I am?'

'The most adorable, lovely girl it has ever been my luck to meet.'

'Oh, shut up,' she said rudely, for she hated that sort of talk which she never believed to be sincere.

'*Luz de mi vida*, must you always trample on my heart?'

Laurel knew she attracted him, and he enjoyed flirting with her, but he was not serious, else she would not have dared to spend so much time with him.

'It will soon recover, it's a very elastic organ. What about Pilar in Malaga and Maddalena in Torremolinos?'

'But I may never be alone with them,' he said mournfully. 'You do not know, Laurel, how formal and tedious Spanish courtship can be. There has to be weeks of bowing and scraping before one may take a girl out, and then one may only hold her hand for five minutes. The *señoritas* know the drill and insist upon it being followed precisely, though they are becoming more accommodating now. Foreign competition has broken their monopoly.'

'Poor Esteban,' she said mockingly, 'but if all this lengthy ritual has to take place, Luis may still be in the early stages, and therefore your mother has no cause for anxiety.'

'But the suitor must present himself nearly every day, and Luis has not been to Sevilla since Cristina returned from Madrid.'

'Oh, really?' Laurel tried not to feel elated by this information. The last thing she wanted to do was to come between Luis and his prospective bride—correction, she was willing herself to be-

lieve that, but jealousy could not be entirely eliminated. At times she hated poor Cristina, whom
she had never met, for being all the things she
herself was not.

Esteban observed: 'A Spanish woman's pride
will not permit her to reproach a faithless lover,
but she might stick a knife into him, given the
opportunity.'

'But are Luis and Cristina, I mean Señorita
Ordoñez, lovers?'

'Only metaphorically speaking. Too bad if another Aguilas jilts the lady, and for the same
reason,' he grinned mischievously. 'Pale gold
hair.'

'Don't talk nonsense,' she said crossly, for she
was finding the subject painful; if Luis was neglecting his intended it was not because of her.

'It is not nonsense. You and your sister have a
lot to answer for. The Lester lure seems to be
irresistible to the Aguilas. Pedro, Luis, myself
have all been caught by it.'

Laurel swung her legs off the couch and stood
up.

'I'm not going to stay here any longer and listen
to you . . .'

'What was that about the Lester lure?' said a
deep voice behind her. Laurel's heart gave a leap
and she clutched her scanty robe more closely
round her. She did not look round as Esteban
replied jokingly:

'An apt description, do you not agree, *mi her-
mano*?'

'Very.' Luis' tone was dry.

Laurel swung round, lovely colour suffusing her tanned cheeks, blue eyes sparkling.

'Are you trying to insult me too?'

He was either on his way to, or returning from some business assignation, for he was immaculately dressed—lightweight fawn trousers, holland jacket, white silk shirt and black tie, which he still wore for Pedro. By contrast, his hair and eyes looked blacker than ever, and he was burned to the colour of teak by the sun.

'I think Esteban meant a compliment, not an insult,' he returned mildly. 'Little witch,' he added below his breath, his eyes sliding over her long bare legs.

'Then be careful I don't put a spell on you,' she said daringly, as excitement stirred in her under his scrutiny.

'You have,' he said simply.

'There, what did I tell you?' Esteban cried triumphantly. 'Mercedes was right.'

'I do not know what Mercedes has been saying, but it was probably inaccurate and unpleasant,' Luis retorted. He turned to Laurel, who though she knew she ought to retreat was loath to leave his presence. 'Your swimming is coming along well, Esteban is to be congratulated on his pupil.'

'Do you mean you've been watching me? When? How?'

'My suite overlooks the pool, remember? I found the spectacle diverting.'

He had never appeared on the balcony, so she

had had no idea that he had been there, watching from the interior, like an animal in its lair. Her efforts had not always been very dignified, and had certainly not been intended as an amusement for him. She said stiffly:

'I should have thought you would have had better things to do.'

He shook his head, laughing at her dismay, a flash of white teeth in his dark face.

'Would you deny me such an innocent pleasure? You look charming in only a swimsuit, but might I suggest a bikini might be even better? You can buy them in Fuengirola, two little wisps of material.'

'Oh, you!' She clenched her fists. She did not know him in this mood, teasing, mocking, two little derisory devils dancing in his jet black eyes.

'That is a very good idea,' Esteban agreed, brown eyes alight with mischief. 'You can probably get them in Mijas. I will help you choose what suits you.'

'You will do nothing of the sort,' Laurel told him coldly. 'And if you two can't talk sensibly, I'm going in.'

'What can I say to please you?' Esteban asked reproachfully. 'If I compliment you, you say shut up, if I offer my assistance, you threaten to desert me. They are bringing out the lunch, can we all have it here together?'

'I am afraid I cannot stay for it.' Luis' manner changed to chill formality. 'I have an appointment in Sevilla.'

His eyes met Laurel's, and now they were hard as frozen tar. She felt as if a cold wind had blown over her.

'Courting?' Esteban asked flippantly.

'Mind your own business,' Luis snapped. '*Adios.*'

They watched the tall lithe figure stride away and vanish into the hotel.

'So that is why he was all dressed up,' Esteban commented. He glanced compassionately at Laurel. 'I am afraid he has taken Mama's warning to heart.'

'It doesn't worry me what he does,' Laurel told him with a fine assumption of indifference. 'Would you mind if I went in? I ... I've got a headache coming on, the sun is so strong.'

'No, *querida*,' he said gently, 'but I would like to say this, I would rather have you for a sister than that stuck-up piece in Sevilla, whatever Mercedes says.'

Laurel smiled wanly. 'Thank you, Esteban, but don't talk about impossibilities. I'm sure if you think about it, you won't want *another* English sister-in-law.'

'You are quite different from Joanna,' he said quickly.

'You can't be sure. Be seeing you!'

Esteban watched her walk away with an un-characteristically troubled look in his merry eyes.

Forestalling Laurel's request for a puppy for Peter, Doña Elvira had given him a dog, not what Laurel would have chosen, but a white poodle

bitch. She was to be his very own, his grandmother told him, but of course he could not take
her into the hotel. Later on, Fifi and Pom-pom
would mate and then there would be little ones.
Rather to Laurel's surprise, these Spaniards had
no inhibitions about discussing the facts of life.
Peter was charmed with the idea, but as Laurel
had not seen Fifi, she must come and be introduced.

She promised to come one morning when his
Spanish lesson was over, and duly presented herself. There was no one about, and since she was
no stranger, she walked in and knocked on the
salón door, expecting Peter would be with his
grandmother. Guessing who it was, he flew to
open the door, and too late she realised there was
a visitor, while she hastily excused herself,
Mercedes, who was present, said in English to
the stranger:

'It is Pedro's nursemaid, she has come to fetch
him.'

This description was meant to humiliate her,
but Peter thwarted her object.

'She's not,' he cried, 'she's my *tia*, same as
you.'

'Of course,' Doña Elvira intervened. 'Cristina,
may I present Señorita Lester? Laurel, this is the
Señorita Ordoñez.'

On the principal that if the mountain wouldn't
come to Mahomet, Mahomet must go to the
mountain, Mercedes had asked Cristina to stay,
for there *was* a spare room. She expected that the

girl's actual presence would spur her brother into action, and as much as she could feel friendship for anyone, Cristina came into that category.

Cristina held out a flaccid hand, and Laurel touched her fingers. So this was Luis' *novia*. She was as Esteban had described her, dark, handsome, and looked capable of passion. What he had not mentioned was her matt creamy skin and her huge dark eyes. She was short and plump, and would be stout later on if she were not careful, she presented the complete antithesis of the slender English girl with her pale colouring. Her eyes narrowed, as she asked coldly:

'Joanna de las Aguilas' sister, I presume?'

'And very like her,' Mercedes said with emphasis, and she did not mean only in looks.

Cristina was playing with a little lace fan, attached by a ribbon to her wrist. She wore an expensive silk suit patterned in rich dark colours, and very high-heeled black shoes. Her hair was parted in the middle and drawn into a knot on her nape. There were rings on all her fingers and pearl studs in her ears. Laurel's eyes went instinctively to her left hand and she then remembered that meant nothing in Spain and the significant token was a bracelet.

'I hope that you enjoy your visit,' Cristina said politely. She had a strong accent and her English was not very fluent. Her dark eyes expressed animosity, but she could not be expected to feel friendly towards the kin of the woman who had stolen her first *novio*.

'Yes, very much,' Laurel returned mechanically. 'Please forgive me for intruding. I didn't know anyone was here, and Peter wanted me to see his dog.'

'Ah *si*, the English think so much of the dog.'

Peter had picked up the bundle of curly white hair that was sharing Pom-pom's basket.

'Isn't she lovely, Tia, and when I sleep here, Granny lets her come on my bed.'

Granny knew how to wean Peter from Laurel; dogs on beds was something she would not have allowed.

'Unhealthy,' Mercedes muttered acidly.

Peter glared at her. 'Fifi is very clean, and I *like* having her.'

Laurel gently stroked the small head with the tuft on top. To her mind a spaniel or a terrier would have been a better pet for a boy than this little toy, which was too delicate to walk far or play games, but she had her points as a bedfellow.

'Pedro had better go back to lunch with you,' Mercedes decided, 'as we have a visitor.'

'Yes, of course,' Laurel agreed. 'Coming, Peter?'

Peter turned to his grandmother. 'Can't I take Fifi with me? Just while we have lunch?'

'I am afraid not, *chico*, dogs are forbidden in the Reina.'

Laurel was sure the staff would stretch a point and Fifi would be allowed in the garden, but she said nothing. The little animal was the bait to ensure Peter's presence at the Casa, and the

Señora was not going to relinquish her, even for a short while. Peter reluctantly returned Fifi to her basket, and Cristina extended her plump hand towards Laurel.

'*Hast a luego,*' she said languidly.

Again their fingers barely touched. Laurel murmured something about being pleased to have met her, bowed to the other two women and left.

So that was Luis' intended bride, obviously rich, and very Spanish, but Esteban had told her Luis had gone to Barcelona for a couple of days, so there seemed to have been a lack of communication somewhere, but she might be making a long stay.

Entering the foyer, she found Esteban at the desk, flirting with Carmen. He came at once to meet her.

'Been to retrieve the brat?' he asked cheerfully. 'When is he going to be installed at the Casa permanently?'

'Ssh!' But Peter had run to the desk to try out his Spanish on Carmen, with whom he was a favourite. 'Soon, I expect,' she went on in a low voice, 'but I'm still not quite happy about it. He gets on well with your mother, and she's trying to win him with pets.'

'That obnoxious white poodle? He is a boy, she should have bought him a proper dog.'

'Oh, he's charmed with Fifi, and I believe there's a pony on the way, so Luis is going to teach him to ride.'

'You mean I am—Luis will be too busy. Come

and sit down,' he indicated a red velvet-covered bench beside the window looking into the patio. 'I suppose you met my future sister-in-law?'

Laurel sat down wearily, staring at the large pink roses blooming in the patio.

'Yes, but why isn't Luis here to meet her?'

'Because he did not know she was coming. Mercedes' stage management has gone wrong somehow. She meant to give Luis a pleasant surprise. You know she invited her to counteract your pernicious influence, *querida*?'

'Oh, don't start that again—and don't call me dear,' she said irritably. She knew what the word meant now.

Esteban addressed the ceiling. 'She has the face of an angel, and the tongue of an asp! I suppose you have had a trying morning, I do not imagine you found Cristina any more to your taste than she did you.'

'Was it likely we'd discover we were soulmates? Don't forget, Joanna was my sister, and she'll never forgive that.' Laurel smiled wanly. 'But it's your sister I'm worried about with regard to Peter—I'm afraid her dislike of me extends to him.'

'Because he takes after you and his mother. You should have darkened his skin and dyed his hair before you produced him. She hated Joanna and made mischief between her and Pedro.'

Laurel looked at him quickly. 'I'm afraid my poor sister was not always discreet.'

He shrugged his shoulders. 'Best let bygones

be bygones. But she believes you are another of the same sort, and of course you are in love with Luis.'

'I'm not!' she cried, then meeting his shrewd gaze: 'Well, yes, I suppose I am. Oh, God, Esteban, is it obvious?'

'No, but inevitable,' he returned seriously. 'Luis is like a flypaper to flies where women are concerned, but do not distress yourself—I am sure only I have seen it, and that is because I am a little in love with you myself, but it was very foolish of you to let yourself be caught.'

'Do you imagine I wanted to fall for him?' Laurel asked in a low tense voice, for the first time admitting what she had tried to disguise from herself. She realised now that she well and truly had fallen in love with Luis. She made a little helpless gesture. 'I know it's quite hopeless.'

'Do not make a tragedy out of it,' he admonished her. 'Me, I have been in and out of love many times, and when the lady is unkind, I console myself by reflecting that it will pass and there are ... what do you say, many more fishes swimming about.'

Laurel wished she had his facile nature. His love affairs did not go very deep, and to use his metaphor, there were not many fish of Luis' calibre swimming about.

'Do you think Cristina will make him happy?' she asked.

Again he shrugged. '*Quién sabe?* She has all the attributes he requires in a wife. She will give him a quiverfull of nice little black-haired, black-eyed *niños* full of nice blue blood.' Their eyes met. '*Dios*, Laurel why does it have to be so, why cannot you follow your hearts?'

Laurel sighed. She knew where her own heart was leading, but she was not at all sure about Luis'.

'Because it's not done in Andalucia,' she said bitterly.

'It was once . . .'

'And you know what happened. That should be an object lesson to me, shouldn't it?' She touched his hand. 'You're the most human of the Aguilas, Esteban, and I thank you for your sympathy, but I'll be all right. I'll get over it. When I get back to England I'll take your advice and look out for a suitable, ordinary Englishman, of my own standing, and all this,' she indicated the rose-filled patio, the beautiful marble foyer, 'will seem a dream.'

'I wish you luck,' he said gently, 'but it seems a pity. You and Luis at Ronda, you made such a charming couple.'

Laurel winced. 'Ah, please don't remind me of that.' She forced a shaky laugh. 'Are you coming over all romantic? We must be practical, and shouldn't you be paying your respects to Señorita Ordoñez?'

'It is not I she wants to see, and I do not like hen parties,' he returned flippantly. He sprang lightly to his feet. 'Let us go and find some lunch. Hi, Pedrillo,' he called, 'as you say in your delightful vernacular, grub's up.'

Peter came running and they went down the marble staircase, and out into the sunlit garden, where the buffet was spread beneath the trees.

Luis came back looking more saturnine than ever, but Laurel hardly saw him at all. He was, she presumed, spending all his spare time at the Casa, courting Cristina, who was in no hurry to leave.

The pony arrived and was stabled near the hotel. What with his Spanish lessons, riding, swimming and Fifi, Laurel was less and less necessary to Peter. He spent more and more nights at the Casa, saying he liked having his own room and Fifi. Sometimes he seemed to forget she was there.

Laurel decided it was time for her to go. She had accomplished what she had come to do, established Peter with his Spanish relatives, and though he would inevitably miss her ... at first, he had plenty of other distractions. Though she saw so little of Luis, he was constantly in her mind, and she was always hoping for a chance encounter. She would know no real peace until she had left his vicinity, and, as she had told Esteban, her sojourn in Spain back in London would seem like a dream.

But she had a problem. She had not got enough money for her return fare. It had been tacitly understood that that was to be provided when she left, it was part of the contract, but the Aguilas seemed to have forgotten about it. She needed

what she had to keep her until she found work
again upon her return, and she might well find
she was redundant when she applied to her old
firm for re-employment. She hated having to ask,
but it was foolish to be so sensitive when she really
needed the money, which was a mere fleabite to
the wealthy Aguilas.

So, pocketing her pride, she went to see Doña
Elvira.

The Señora received her coldly, she was jealous
of Peter's affection for her, but she brightened up
when Laurel explained her need.

'Of course you must have it, and we will make
all arrangements for your journey, but you will
have to ask Luis about it. He manages all the
financial affairs for the family, and I daresay,' the
shrewd eyes narrowed, 'he will add a little bonus.
He, like the rest of us, appreciates your action in
bringing Pedrillo to us, and would like to show it
in a practical manner.'

'I only want what's due to me,' Laurel told her
stiffly, resenting the elder woman's manner. She
knew Doña Elvira was dying to be rid of her, but
she need not humiliate her by talking as if she
were paying off a servant. Would Luis take the
same attitude? It would be painful if he did, and
she was after all Peter's aunt.

Doña Elvira unbent a little.

'You must not think we are ungrateful, the boy
has given me a new interest in life, but we cannot
continue to impose upon your kindness. You have
your own life to lead and it would be as well if

you took it up again.' The eagle eyes were full of meaning. The Señora was not stupid, she saw most of what was going on around her, though she rarely left the house. She added with emphasis: 'Believe me, my dear, there is nothing for you here in Spain.'

Nothing . . . and everything.

Laurel took her leave.

CHAPTER SEVEN

LAUREL had been hesitant about approaching Doña Elvira, but she was ten times more reluctant to go to Luis. In vain she reminded herself of his assurances that he looked upon her as a relative, felt responsible for her and had even offered her a villa, so would be co-operative in the small matter of her return fare. He had been so distant of late, she feared she had unintentionally offended him, though she could not think how. The withered remains of his rose she had put away in a little cardboard box. Though she derided herself for being so sentimental, she could not bear to throw it away.

She hoped Doña Elvira would give him a hint, but several days passed without anything happening. She thought of asking Esteban to make her request for her, then scorned herself for being a coward. She only wanted what was her due, and Luis would not press her to stay. Perhaps that was it, it would hurt her to see unconcealed relief when she told him she wanted to leave; possibly he had forgotten she was still in his hotel.

She dressed herself in her black dress, and decided not to put on any make-up. She looked pale and wan, the heat, and it had become very hot, was sapping her vitality, even her hair was

losing its lustre. Looking in her mirror, she
decided she looked anything but seductive, and
that was her aim. Luis must not imagine she had
wanted to contact him for any reason other than
business. This might be the last time she would
see him, she thought sadly; he would give her the
money and instruct Leonardo the manager to
book her flight and order her taxi, and that would
be that. She would leave as unobtrusively as possible, and it would be best not to say goodbye to
Peter; it would be too harrowing for both of them.
She would suggest to Luis that he tell him, when
she had gone, that she had had to return to
England for a while, and he need not say outright
that she was not coming back. Peter adored his
uncle and he would be the best person to comfort
him.

Having ascertained previously that Luis would
be working in his suite that evening, she
summoned up her courage and went to face him.

'*Entre,*' he called curtly, in answer to her timid
knock.

He was sitting at his desk, with a mass of papers
spread before him. As the night was so warm, he
had discarded his jacket, and was wearing a
short-sleeve silk shirt, open at the neck, and his
sweat-dampened hair fell in wisps over his face as
he pored over the figures he was working upon.
It and his informal garb made him look younger,
and increased his attraction. Laurel looked hastily
away from the sight of his bare muscular
forearms, and the brown column of his throat,

aware that her pulse had quickened.

'Laurel!' he exclaimed when he saw her, pushing the hair out of his eyes and springing to his feet. He reached for his jacket, and she said hastily:

'No, don't put it on, it's so hot. I hope I'm not disturbing you, but I have to ask you something.'

They had not been alone since Ronda, and after Cristina's coming she had only seen him in the distance.

'Sit down,' he indicated the settee by the window where she had sat before . . . and wept. How long ago that seemed. 'Let me get you a drink.'

She shook her head. 'No, thank you.'

'Sit down,' he repeated. 'I cannot talk to you when you stand like a bird poised for flight; do you think I am going to eat you?'

Laurel laughed shakily, 'No, of course not,' and obediently sat. Ignoring her refusal he poured out a glass of Manzanilla, the wine of Seville.

'Drink it,' he ordered, as he brought it to her. 'You look as though you need it. You are very pale, Laurelita,' she flinched at the affectionate diminutive. 'Is anything wrong?'

'Oh, no.' She put the glass down on the small table beside the settee. 'It's only the heat.'

She noticed there were roses in a vase on his desk, red roses, the roses of Ronda, but the maid would have put them there, they held no significance for him.

He sat down in the armchair opposite to her,

his eyes intent upon her face.

'*Bien*, what is this great matter that has led you to beard the ogre in his den?'

So he had sensed her trepidation and was making a joke of it.

'Oh, nothing very important. I've decided it is time for me to leave, and your mother said I must ask you for my fare, which it was agreed . . .' She stopped.

For Luis had sprung to his feet, as if he had been shot.

'You cannot go, Laurelita, I will not let you go!'

His vehemence took her aback.

'But, Luis, I must. Peter will be all right now. He has so many other interests, he'll not miss me after the first wrench. I . . . I can't stay here for ever.'

She saw she had taken him completely by surprise, but hadn't his mother mentioned her departure? Apparently not. He said more calmly:

'I thought you would stay here for the summer, or until Pedrillo goes to school. Why do you want to leave so soon?'

'Because there really isn't any reason to stay,' she said wearily; she had not expected he would question the necessity for her to leave. 'I've done what I came for, got Peter settled, and now, as Doña Elvira has told me, it's time I went back and took up my old life again.'

'You have discussed this with Mama, without speaking to me?'

'I didn't want to bother you about such a small matter, but when I asked her for my fare she said I must apply to you.'

'Small matter!' he ejaculated. There was an ominous glitter in his eyes, and she felt vaguely afraid. Why was he making it so difficult for her?

'Oh, Luis, please let me go,' she said desperately. 'Nobody wants me here.'

'I do.' The words were wrenched out of him, almost it seemed against his will. Laurel felt a surge of joy at the admission, but she quickly quelled it. She could not stay exposed to the ever-present danger of an emotional outburst, and with Cristina across the way, it would be shockingly reprehensible. Surely he must see that? She said steadily:

'Then that is another reason why I must go.'

'I cannot let you go,' he repeated distractedly. 'I could not bear never to see you again, you little white witch.' He moved restlessly about the room, then halted in front of her, and his expression was menacing.

'Is it because of that man in England—you hinted that there was one—that you are determined to go?'

Laurel had completely forgotten that she had tried to mislead him with her arch, 'Possibly,' in reply to a similar question. She looked blank, and then realised that he had shown her a way of escape. He would release her if she could convince him she was involved elsewhere.

'Yes,' she lied. 'James . . .' she mentioned the

first name that came into her head, 'declares I've been away too long. It isn't fair to him,' she was improvising wildly, 'when he didn't want me to come away in the first place.'

'You have kept very quiet about him.' Luis was looking at her suspiciously. 'You gave me to understand you were alone in the world.'

'Well, I'm not engaged yet,' she was pleating her skirt nervously. 'We have a ... an understanding.' She forced a little laugh. 'It would be unwise to leave him too long, he may take up with someone else!'

But she had made a mistake, for she had aroused the fiery jealousy of the Spanish temperament. She had already thrown Luis out of gear by announcing her imminent departure for which he had not been prepared, and now her innocent little deception had driven him beyond his control. His black eyes suddenly blazed, and he almost snarled:

'You shall not go to this ... this James, not after what has been between us. *Dios*, have I held off, suffered the torments of the damned, to surrender you to another man?'

He swooped. Laurel was pulled up into his arms, crushed against his chest, while his hard, demanding lips claimed hers. All her good resolutions and scruples were swept away as the dam of their pent emotions broke and engulfed them in a fiery flood. Laurel clung to him, her arms about his neck, her fingers entwined in his hair. Impatiently he pulled down the back zip of her dress, and it fell away, exposing her creamy shoulders. His mouth drew trails of fire over her neck and bosom, causing her shivers of delight. She clung closer to his long lean length feeling his thighs pressing against hers. Lifting his head, he said hoarsely, the words punctuated by hard breaths:

'And you . . . ask me to pay . . . to send you away!'

Laurel, drowned in sensation, was past all reasoning thought. She laid her cheek against the opening in his shirt, flesh against bare flesh, and closed her eyes in ecstasy.

Luis whispered thickly in her ear:

'There is only one ending to all this.'

He lifted her in his arms and turned towards his bedroom. Laurel was incapable of any resistance. She wanted what was to come as much as he did. Why should she object?

The telephone rang . . . and continued to ring. An insistent summons, that instrument that is the harbinger of news good or bad. Lovers rush to it, full of eager anticipation, others are impatient of interruption, or apprehensive of disaster, but few can resist its urgency, certainly not Luis, conditioned by habit and business training. He halted by the desk, allowing Laurel to slide to her feet, but retaining one arm about her, as he reached for the phone with his free hand, automatically putting it to his ear.

'Damn you, what is it?' he growled.

Laurel could hear the deferential Spanish voice

from reception. She leaned against Luis wrapped
in a sensuous dream. He would dispose of the
interruption and then they would be alone together.

Luis dropped the receiver back on to its cradle
with a Spanish oath. He withdrew his arm and
became galvanised into hasty action.

'Mercedes and Cristina are in reception,' he
said harshly, reaching for his jacket. 'They are
coming up.'

The dream was shattered. Laurel ran towards
the door, intent only upon escape, but Luis' hand
on her shoulder stopped her.

'Are you crazy? You cannot go rushing into the
corridor looking as though I have raped you!' He
pulled up the zip of her dress. 'Sit down on the
settee and compose yourself. We have a few
minutes while they are exchanging compliments
with Leonardo.'

He had shrugged into his jacket and was fasten-
ing a black cravat about his neck. Feeling dazed,
Laurel on the settee was mechanically adjusting
her dress, and smoothing her hair. It was lucky
she had not used any make-up, there were no
smudged lips, or telltale marks on Luis' shirt. The
glass of Manzanilla was still beside her. Luis was
using a pocket comb to bring order to his hair,
listening for sounds in the passage. Laurel would
have given a lot to avoid the coming ordeal, but if she
left now, she would meet the intruders on the stairs,
and she was feeling shaky. Better to stay where she
was and allow Luis to do the explaining.

Hearing footsteps, he threw the door open with a flourish, saying in Spanish:

'Welcome, dear ladies, I am honoured that you have come to call upon me.'

Luis had completely recovered his poise. In a few moments he had transformed from a man consumed by passion into his normal suave self. But Laurel still felt churned up inside, and her hands were trembling so much she had to clasp them firmly in her lap. She wondered vaguely what Luis was going to say.

They came in, Mercedes severe in a shapeless black dress, Cristina in red brocade with a lace shawl about her shoulders and diamonds at her throat. The former glanced malevolently at Laurel, but showed no surprise, Cristina looked astonished and said something to Luis in a hard metallic voice in her own tongue. Luis smiled serenely and explained in English:

'Señorita Lester came to see me about arrangements for her return to England. But do sit down, Cristina,' he indicated the armchair opposite to Laurel which he had previously occupied himself. 'Let me get you a drink.'

Mercedes said icily: 'Mama and I have been wondering when she was going—we have decided the boy would do better without her disturbing influence. She keeps him reminded of all the things we want him to forget.'

She had seated herself upon the only upright chair in the room, a wooden one with a hard seat.

Mercedes was never happy unless she was uncomfortable and making other people feel the same.

'But it is I who make the decisions,' Luis returned blandly, while Laurel flushed at his sister's contemptuous tone.

'Then surely you see the wisdom of dismissing her.' Mercedes had noticed Laurel's agitation and drawn her own conclusions.

'Laurel is not a servant to be dismissed,' he rebuked her. 'She is an honoured guest, and I have been telling her I do not consider Pedrillo can do without her yet and I hope she will spend the rest of the summer with us.'

Laurel glanced at him quickly. He could not mean that—her position was becoming far too difficult; he had only said it to needle Mercedes, who was looking like a cobra coiled to strike. He turned to Cristina.

'*Que tal, querida*, I have not seen you all day.'

'Is why I ask Mercedes to bring me here,' she said eagerly. 'I wish to see where you live and work.' She looked up at him reproachfully. 'You hide away like a hermit. Is not kind when I am here!'

Standing beside her, he patted her shoulder, telling her he had been very busy, indicating the papers on his desk, but he was glad she had interrupted him, she was a most welcome diversion, but he spoke absently, and Laurel realised he was not as composed as he was trying to appear, a muscle twitched in his cheek, and he clenched and unclenched the hand farthest from Cristina. She rose to her feet:

'If you'll excuse me, I'll go now.' She was glad to find her voice was steady. She met Luis' eyes over Cristina's head and saw they were still smouldering. He told her:

'You must not let these ladies drive you away. They will be grieved if you depart.' (She knew they were longing to see the back of her.) 'You have not drunk your wine.' A mocking glint came into his eyes. 'You and Cristina should get to know each other, you have so much in common.' (Himself?) 'Sit down again and let us enjoy a little pleasant conversation.'

He went to pour the wine for Cristina, he knew Mercedes did not drink, and Laurel meekly subsided upon the settee, feeling as if she and Cristina were puppets he was manipulating, as perhaps they were. Politeness necessitated staying a little longer, after what he had said. Luis brought the wine to Cristina and looked from one to the other of the two girls.

'The red rose and the white,' he almost purred, 'such a charming contrast, both lovely and both sweet.'

What was his object in keeping her there, Laurel wondered, and paying fulsome compliments—did he know he was tormenting her, or was he doing it deliberately to pay her back for her supposed lover in England? He could be cruel sometimes.

'Is insipid, the white rose,' Cristina declared.

She understood this flowery talk, it was what she expected. She gave Luis a languishing glance. '*Los hombres*, prefer the red, do they not?'

'You should know,' Luis returned gallantly. 'British girls, Cristina, are cold, because they live under grey skies, they are afraid to love, unlike the red rose, which spreads its petals to welcome the sun.'

How could he say that, even to reassure Cristina, when she had only a short while ago been ready to open her petals to receive his love? And why the simile of roses when that flower would always recall to her that day in Ronda when he had been so different from this mocking devil who seemed determined to wound her? Laurel could only surmise that in some way she had offended him, perhaps because she wanted to leave, or said she did, for she knew she would leave her heart behind in Mijas.

Cristina tilted her head coquettishly, opening her fan, which as usual was attached to her wrist. Holding it over the lower part of her face, she looked coyly at Luis over its rim. Laurel had heard there was a language of fans, but it did not take much skill to interpret Cristina's action as an invitation. The Spanish girl had been practising feminine wiles ever since she was out of her cradle, and Luis seemed to be enjoying her byplay, and he needed to allay any suspicions Mercedes might have planted in her jealous mind. It occurred to Laurel that he was keeping her there to demonstrate to his intended his indifference to her, and to remind her that the chaste, protected Spanish girl was his choice for his consort, while Laurel was only a plaything, to be taken up and discarded at his whim. Thwarted by this unexpected visit, he was venting his frustration in barbed talk, not caring how much he hurt her, for he must know that she had been frustrated too and was yearning for him with every fibre of her being.

She was unconscious that her eyes were betraying her as she gazed wistfully at Luis. Luis and Cristina, apparently absorbed in each other, did not notice, but Mercedes did. As she sat apart on her hard chair, her keen observant eyes took in every nuance. She had known her brother, boy and man, all his life, and she understood him far better than either of the other two women did, and what she was seeing disquieted her.

'In England the manners are much more free?' Cristina was saying, and Laurel knew she was recalling that she had found her alone with Luis.

'Very much so,' Luis assured her. 'To Laurel there is nothing unconventional about coming to see me alone, and we often need to confer about the boy, who is our joint nephew.'

Mercedes snorted. 'Hardly necessary, but Luis has his reasons for being very interested in that child, who is so unlike his father.' Luis shot her a warning look, and she smiled sourly. 'From which you may deduce, my dear Cristina, that he will make an excellent father himself.'

'If he ever marry a wife,' Cristina said mournfully, thereby betraying that Luis had not yet proposed to her.

'Only fools rush into matrimony,' Luis stated casually. 'It is something that needs careful consideration.'

Cristina looked furious, and Laurel felt sorry for her, for such a remark was not to be expected from an ardent suitor. She did not think Cristina was in love with Luis, there was no softness in her eyes when she looked at him, but he could give her a fine establishment, and she wanted to make sure of him, and it. She said something in Spanish, her eyes snapping, and Luis smiled quizzically, if she were reproaching him, he was quite unmoved.

'*Paciencia, querida,*' he told her. 'All will resolve itself in time.'

When he had had his way with her, Laurel thought, but she had had a revulsion of feeling. She was thankful now for the telephone call that had saved her from her madness. She was in love with Luis and longed for his love in return, but if he had any to give he would bestow it upon his countrywoman. A brief physical satisfaction was all she could expect herself, which would have left her feeling degraded and bereft, for she could not kid herself that Luis had any intention of establishing a permanent relationship with her. What had happened that evening had been unpremeditated, an upsurge of the violent emotion which could so easily erupt between them, but it had not changed anything, except to make her departure all the more urgent.

Cristina was whispering to Luis now, behind her fan, his head bent towards her, and from his expression he was amused. Sitting with these three Spaniards, more or less ignored, Laurel had never felt more alien or more alone. She drank the wine in her glass, but did not taste it. Now she had finished it, surely he would allow her to depart.

'I really must go now,' she said with forced brightness. 'I've some letters to write.'

A polite excuse, because she had no one to whom to write. She caught Luis' baleful eyes, and knew he was thinking 'to James'. But there was no James. However, he did not try to detain her, and she politely shook hands with the two un-responsive women, amid a murmuring of good-nights. Luis opened the door for her, and as she passed him she said appealingly:

'You know I must go, Luis, so you will attend to the little matter about which I asked you?'

'We will speak further about it,' he returned uncompromisingly. '*Buenas noches.*'

He did not offer his hand, and intuitively she knew that he dared not touch her.

She went swiftly down the corridor without looking back, for she felt he was watching her.

She did not at all want a further interview with him, and prayed he would see about her ticket without a further request. He *must* realise that the only sensible course was to let her return to England. His womenfolk, all three of them, would

press the matter, and she was confident he would
yield to their persuasions, but never had her
future appeared more bleak and friendless.

Next morning, Cristina left the Casa; Laurel,
who was in her room at the time, saw her go. She
was travelling, not in Luis' car, but a hired one.
Mercedes and Doña Elvira were seeing her off,
and there was a great deal of excited chatter while
the servant piled her gear into the boot of the car.
Neither of the men was present. The three women
embraced, Cristina was handed into the car and
driven off. Laurel knew Esteban was spending the
day in Malaga, but Luis must be somewhere
around, and it was strange he had not come to say
goodbye to his *novia*, if she were that, nor had
anybody said last night that she was leaving,
unless that had been her real reason for coming to
his suite, and they made their farewells after she
herself had left.

Laurel hung about the vestibule and lounge,
hoping to receive word that arrangements had
been made for her own departure, for she was
confident that upon reflection Luis would agree
to it. Once she asked Leonardo if there were any
message for her. He looked blank—was she expecting one? If so, it would be delivered *pronto*.
Knowing the Spanish tendency to procrastinate,
she steeled herself to wait, but now she knew she
had to go, she was impatient to be away.

She went outside for lunch; though she was not
hungry, it served to pass the time. The attendant
always reserved for her a mattress set in the shade

to the side of the buffet, in a secluded corner surrounded by the steep banks that enclosed the upper part of the garden. Umbrellas were put up every morning, and one of these was set over her couch. The waiter was very attentive to her and she must give him a substantial tip when she left. The sun beat down out of a cloudless sky, and the distant view was obscured by a heat haze. The pool was full of near-naked visitors and the waiters were running back and forth with iced drinks. Laurel had a clear sight of it from the open side of her retreat.

Peter came to join her; he too was tanned to a lovely brown, and he was growing fast. He had passed his fifth birthday, the pony had been Luis' present, and she had given him some gear for it. She had been invited to the Casa for lunch in honour of the day, a rather formal meal at which Luis had been present, but afterwards he had taken the boy down to the sea. Laurel had not been invited to go with them—that had been before Cristina arrived. Peter was going to be a tall man, and Laurel wondered if he would become darker as the years past. It seemed to her his hair had already become less blond since they had come, but his eyes, so similar to hers, would always be blue.

'Awful shindig last night,' he told her, sitting at the foot of her mattress. He giggled. 'Spanish sounds so funny when people get excited, pop-pop-pop.' He had been spending the night at the Casa.

'What was it about?'

He spread his hands—he was acquiring Latin gestures.

'I don't know, I'd gone to bed, but you could hear them all over the house. Fifi barked. Tio Luis was there, I know his voice, and this morning Granny—I mean Abuela—was very, very cross.'

So there had been a row, with the result that Cristina had flounced off to Seville that morning without Luis saying goodbye. Laurel hoped she had not been the cause of it, but if she had, they would soon make it up when she was out of the way. If only Luis would produce her air ticket!

'Do you want to do anything?' she asked, hoping he would not suggest anything energetic.

'Dunno, it's so hot, and there are too many people in the pool to have a swim. Oh, here is Tio Luis.'

He brightened and ran to meet his uncle.

Laurel sat up and pulled down the skirt of her yellow sun dress over her legs. At last he was coming to tell her he had made the necessary arrangements. He was wearing white trousers and shirt, his jacket slung over one shoulder. Her stomach muscles contracted, and excitement stirred in her veins. Last night they had . . . but she must *not* think about last night. She must accept her dismissal and forget the might-have-beens. Halting beside her, he asked Peter to bring him a chair, and the boy rushed off to procure one of the white metal ones from the buffet. They exchanged banal greetings, mere meaningless words, but his eyes were intent and searching, and hers were luminous. Her hair gleamed around her face, and she looked very young and appealing as she gazed up into his dark, enigmatical face. Peter lugged up the chair and Luis thanked him gravely. Dropping his jacket on the grass, he seated himself beside her and turned to Peter. There would have been plenty of room on the mattress beside her, but she surmised he considered that would be too intimate.

'I want to talk to your aunt,' he told the boy, and then, seeing his face fall, 'but I will take you down to the coast when I have finished. Go and plague Carmen, she is not busy and it is cooler indoors.'

Peter went reluctantly, and Laurel said:

'You're very good to him.'

He was watching Peter's retreat, and he returned absently:

'He is a fine little chap, it is a pity . . .' He broke off and turned his head to look down into the blue eyes raised to his, which were so exactly like Peter's.

'It is time you came clean,' he told her. 'Of course I realise he is your child.'

CHAPTER EIGHT

LAUREL returned the stare of the black eyes probing into hers, wondering if the heat had addled his brains or hers, or if she had heard aright.

'You look as though you could not tell a lie to save your life,' he told her. 'But you are as two-faced as your sister was, and I have been as gullible as poor Pedro until Mercedes brought me to my senses last night. The boy told me himself that he was known as Peter Lester in England.'

'Well, Joanna reverted to her maiden name, and yours is a bit of a mouthful . . .' Then it hit her. 'Oh, no, Luis, you can't be suggesting we swapped babies, that sort of thing only occurs in third-rate melodramas. Why ever should I want to do such a thing?'

'To obtain security for him,' he said gently. 'I do not blame you, Laurel—with your upbringing, you are not likely to be scrupulous, and you saw an opportunity that you could not resist to provide for him. Last night . . .' He looked away from her, 'Cristina and I . . . quarrelled about you. I told her . . . never mind what. Then Mercedes talked to me, she said I was infatuated—perhaps I was.' He passed his hand wearily over his face. 'She never did believe your story, and neither did I . . . at first.'

Which accounted for his initial antagonism, those penetrating looks that had disconcerted her, his occasional strange remarks. He had thought she might be a fraud.

'You and your charming sister are just blind prejudiced,' she cried angrily, cut to the quick that he could so misjudge her. 'Because Peter used his mother's name . . .'

'Wait a moment, spitfire,' his smile was almost tender. 'We had only your word, remember, and perhaps you do not know that Joanna wrote to Pedro telling him his son had died . . . of measles and 'flu.'

'That's an invention! Joanna would never write to Pedro, she would have been terrified of giving him a clue to her whereabouts.'

'We have the letter, you can see it if you wish. She thought she would finally put an end to Pedro's quest for the boy. Incidentally, the post-mark was that of a part of London where she was *not* hiding.'

The bright sunlight danced before Laurel's eyes. Such an action was typical of Joanna, obsessed and unbalanced as she became, but she had not dared to tell her sister what she had done. The Aguilas had accepted her communication as truth, but without the confirmation of a copy of the death certificate it was valueless. She told Luis so.

'We knew that, and Mama was convinced the information was false, Joanna's motive being obvious. Pedro promised he would make enquiries, but before he got anywhere, and he was beginning to lose interest in the fate of his son, he was killed. Mama was prostrated by the shock of his death, and was ill for a long time. When your letter came it had the effect of a reviving tonic. We tried to persuade her to wait, to allow me to go to London to interview you and test your veracity, but she insisted you must come at once. She could not bear to think that Pedro's child might be in want.'

So he had come to meet her, full of suspicion and doubt. Couldn't Joanna have foreseen how her foolish letter might reflect upon Peter, and she must have forgotten it when she had asked Laurel to return him to his people—typical of her sister, who never foresaw anything and always acted upon the impulse of the moment.

'But Peter knows he's lost his mother, he calls me Tia.'

'Which would not convey much to the average Briton. Strange that it is the only Spanish word he remembered. He is too young to recall events before his illness, and it was after that I suppose you met your James. By the way, what is his second name?'

Still in shock from Luis' accusations, she answered mechanically: 'B ... Baron.' She had nearly said Bond. Why had she dredged up a name at all, when there was no such person? Was she still trying to delude herself he could be some sort of protection?

'Perhaps you wanted to appear respectable to

this Señor Baron?' Luis said insinuatingly. 'The bereaved mother would have been happy to pass the child off as hers, and hear him call her Mummy, besides she was much indebted to you.'

Laurel made a gesture as if pushing cobwebs away from her face. He was trying to make the improbably sound plausible. Mercedes must have worked hard to think up all this rubbish, for Luis would not by himself have arrived at such feminine conclusions.

'This is ridiculous,' she told him, trying to speak calmly. 'There are people in London—the doctor who attended Peter and Joanna, our neighbours—who'll explode your theories. I didn't realise I would need to bring my credentials with me, or I'd have done something about it.'

It was not the query about Peter that had wounded her, and she had not had time to examine the depth of her hurt, but the realisation that Luis, the man she had learned to love, had been harbouring such cruel doubts of her and had from their first meeting suspected her of being a fraud and a cheat.

'Naturally I shall make a thorough investigation,' Luis said coldly. 'Unless the boy is legitimate he cannot inherit his father's property.'

That wretched property again, that would become his and Esteban's if he could discredit Peter's claim, which it was to his advantage to do. The Toro Negro—but surely on that day his doubts had been allayed. He would not have allowed the staff to be presented to the boy, if they had not—or would he? She looked up into his dark Spanish face, his unrevealing eyes. To play with her and Peter, lead them on, expecting they would betray themselves, manipulate them as the matador does the bull, before he gives the final thrust, wasn't that characteristic of his devious, cruel mind? She cried out in anguish:

'Oh, Luis, Luis, you can't believe all this nonsense! It's your venomous sister who has invented it. She's always hated me because I resemble Joanna.'

'That was the first thing I noticed about you.'

And had chalked it up against her!

'But you said I had honest eyes,' she reminded him. 'You said I was true.'

Those remarks had puzzled her at the time, but now she understood their import.

A spasm crossed his face. 'You *had* convinced me of that,' he told her gently. 'Until last night. I had thought . . . but no matter.' Voice and expression hardened. 'You had deceived me about this James . . . Baron, did you say? You concealed his existence, letting me suppose . . .' Again he broke off, then resumed, and now his face was like stone, his eyes glittering. 'It was when you showed that you were panting to get back to him, insisting that you return at once, that the scales fell from my eyes.'

That was still rankling, her stupid deception that she had embarked upon as a defence against her vulnerability and his demanding passion. There was no James Baron, he was a myth, but how could she convince him of that now? She must try.

'James——' she began hesitantly, but he cut her short.

'Spare me rhapsodies about the creature. No doubt he is all I am not, English to start with, and you said you would only marry an Englishman after Joanna's fiasco, but she was a bitch, that one, she trapped poor Pedro and then betrayed him. I always thought he was a credulous fool until I nearly fell into the same net myself. But I have come to my senses now.'

Feeling bewildered, Laurel said: 'But Pedro married Joanna, and you are going to marry Señorita Ordoñez.'

'Yes, I am,' he said emphatically. He smiled sardonically. 'She has gone off in a rage, but I have only to go to Sevilla and open my arms, and she will fall into them.'

Stabbed, Laurel remarked bitterly: 'An establishment being more potent than love. You don't love her and she doesn't love you.'

'It is not necessary to love to make a successful marriage, though no doubt you are besotted about your James. Love should come afterwards, if it ever comes at all. Similar backgrounds, shared points of view, family approval are much more important.'

Intuitively she knew that these were the arguments he had used to persuade himself into proposing to Cristina, but what did she care about that, when he had brought such a wicked and unfounded accusation against herself? Mercedes had instigated it, of course; she had sat in the corner of Luis' suite watching them like a venomous spider weaving its web, knowing she held a trump card in poor Jo's hysterical letter, oozing disapproval.

'I was here when Peter was born,' she reminded him. 'Your mother will remember that, though you were away. I could not have been . . . having a baby . . . myself, could I?'

For to support his preposterous misconception, she would have had to be pregnant herself.

'Mercedes has remarked, and indeed we have all noticed, that the *niño* seems very advanced for his years. He could be somewhat older than you pretend. If I remember rightly, Mama told me she tried to persuade you to make a long stay, but you said it was imperative you went back.'

To keep her job, of course, but these affluent Aguilas would not appreciate the urgency of that. She burst out:

'What a tangle of suppositions and improbabilities! You ought to be ashamed of yourself, Luis de las Aguilas, for listening to such rubbish!'

Luis sighed: 'If only it were that!'

Laurel seethed with indignation. He *wanted* to despise her to counteract the attraction which they both knew was between them, and had led to the rift with Cristina, but what about Peter? What was to happen to him while they wrangled about his identity? Was he to be thrown out, lose all his newly acquired possessions because of a soured woman's vindictive spite?

She asked anxiously: 'What are you going to do about Peter?'

Luis had been regarding the people in the pool with an abstracted gaze. Without looking at her, he told her:

'Nothing. He stays here. Would you have me break Mama's heart? You have achieved that much, which is more than you deserve. The poor child is innocent, and must be provided for, though he is no Spaniard. Mama need never know the truth, Mercedes agrees about that, and in any case she will not be with us much longer as she starts her novitiate. He is a bright little lad and worthy of a good education. Who knows?' Luis smiled wryly. 'He may become an excellent hotelier.'

'The Toro Negro,' Laurel said, and he winced. Got you there, she thought with bitter triumph, you meant to acquire that for yourself, but you won't get it, it's going to be Peter's.

She felt as if she had a lump of lead where her heart should be. Her growing love for Luis had been shrivelled by black frost; he had killed her dreams and seemed indifferent to what he had done, for he was idly watching a girl who had come out of the pool, a slim nymph in a bikini, who, becoming conscious of his gaze, preened herself and smiled coquettishly.

She reviewed the people she would contact on her return, the doctor for a start. Joanna had never applied for a child allowance, though they could have done with the money, fearful that Pedro might trace her through that source, but the Health Visitor had dropped in from time to time, much to Joanna's disgust. There was the woman in the flat above theirs who had sometimes baby-sat for them, and her employer could testify she had never been off work long enough to have . . . appendicits. Come to that, a medical examination could prove . . . Good God, had Luis thought of that, and that was why he wanted to make love to her?

'Luis . . .' She had to force out the words. 'When you . . . when we . . . were you meaning to seduce me to prove that . . .' she could not finish.

Luis seemed to rouse himself from some sensual fantasy evoked by the near-naked girl. There was a flicker of sardonic humour in his eyes.

'What happened was spontaneous, nor were you adverse to being seduced, though you should have remembered it was . . . unwise. A good con-spirator should be able to control her emotions.'

'Oh, you!' she choked.

'Mercedes said it was a great pity I had been unable to make sure.'

Mercedes again! He had actually discussed their most intimate moments with his unpleasant sister! Laurel swallowed convulsively.

'Of all the cold-blooded, calculating swine!'

He blinked. 'Not exactly cold-blooded, Laurel. You know I have always wanted you.' He smiled crookedly. 'I had dreams, but . . .' He lifted his head proudly. 'An Aguilas cannot accept another man's leavings. Your James may not be so particular, we know England has a permissive society and divorce is rampant. Now it is to be permitted here, we may follow suit, but I expect chastity and fidelity in the woman I marry.'

He meant Cristina. I hope she plays him false, she thought bitterly, she looked quite capable of cuckolding him, the chauvinistic beast! Aloud she told him:

'As soon as I get back to England, and I can't get there too quickly, I'll collect the evidence . . .'

'You are not going back to England,' he interrupted. 'You will stay here. *I* will carry out the investigation. I am not going to permit you to run around suborning witnesses before I have contacted them.'

'Ah, dear God,' she sighed. 'How much further can you insult me? But there is one witness you won't find, and that's James Baron.'

She hoped he would question that and she could perhaps make him believe the man was a myth, but he said brutally:

'Is that so? Perhaps he is doing time.' Laurel clenched her fist; she would have liked to smash it into his mocking face. Luis went on coolly: 'Mercedes wants me to consult a solicitor, put the matter in his hands, but I prefer to deal with it myself. When I return I will dispose of you as I see fit.'

To the other people in the garden they appeared to be having a cosy chat. The bikini girl was meditating whether she dared to join them. She thought she had seen invitation in Luis' eyes and the blonde girl he was with didn't seem to be making much impact; he didn't look amused and might welcome a change.

Laurel stood up, feeling she could not bear any more.

'You're cruel and unjust, Luis,' she said quietly. 'If Peter were my son, I wouldn't want him to be brought up among people like you, but then of course we would never have come. But as he *is* Pedro's, he must have his birthright. You say I must stay here—very well, but I would ask you to keep out of my sight, because I can't bear your presence.'

Luis gave a half groan. '*Ay mi*, Laurelita, if only we could go back to Ronda!'

'Oh, please,' she cried out in agony, 'don't remind me of that day. You were a different person then.'

He looked up at her and she saw pain reflected in his eyes. Was it possible that believing what he did, he too had been wounded? But no, that could not be. He *wanted* to be convinced she was a fraud and a liar, it would free him from feeling any remorse and justify his conduct.

For a long moment they stared into each other's eyes, reproach in hers, in his an infinite regret.

Then Peter came running towards them.

'Tio Luis, Tio Luis, aren't you ever coming? You've been simply ages talking to Tia!' He tugged at his uncle.

Luis rose to his feet. 'Yes, I am coming. Shall we go down to Algeciras? You can swim there and see the Rock across the water. It will be good to get far away from this place.'

They went off laughing together without a backward glance, but Laurel did not see them go because her eyes were blind with tears.

The bikini girl, disappointed by Luis' departure, dived back into the pool with a loud splash.

Unable to endure the vicinity of the pool where Luis' presence still seemed to linger, Laurel went down into the lower parts of the gardens and wandered aimlessly along its winding paths. Clumps of agaves with their prick-edged leaves grew here and there, cruel and sharp like Luis' tongue. Her mind went over and over again the details of that distressing scene.

The Aguilas attitude was not surprising. They had accepted Joanna's letter as truth, for none of them, except Doña Elvira, had been much concerned about the fate of Pedro's baby. She, hungry for grandchildren, had welcomed the news of his survival with joy, the others with reserve. Fraudulent heirs to property had turned up from time to time, some of them causing famous law suits, and it was unfortunate that Peter showed no likeness to his father. As for herself, no one, not even Pedro, had ever questioned her about her English life, she could have left a whole crèche full of babies behind her when she had joined her sister at the villa, for all they knew, so possibly Luis' doubts were justified, but it was not that

that was tormenting her, it was his callous exploitation of her love. Attracted to her as she had been to him, he had played upon her heart and susceptibilities for his amusement, wooing her as he had done at Ronda, and then turning and rending her when he wearied of the game, deciding it was time he clinched with Cristina and denounced her as an impostor.

The hot blue sky, the scorching sunshine awoke in her a longing for soft grey skies and green fields so different from this burnt-up landscape. Holidaymakers revelled in the sun, but after a while it became monotonous, day after day without change. Laurel desperately wanted to get away, to bury her hurt and humiliation in hard work, but her poverty chained her here, and Luis had decreed she must remain.

Esteban came in search of her, and found her looking distraught, her hair tousled, her face still stained with tears. At the sight of him she turned away. He too was Spanish and believed her to be a fraud, but he hurried after her.

'Laurel, stop!' He took hold of her arm. 'Come and sit down.' He guided her to a stone bench and with his own clean handkerchief wiped her eyes. 'What has happened?' His brow darkened. 'Has someone . . . er . . . insulted you? If he has I will kill him!'

He looked so ferocious, she laughed on a note of hysteria.

'No one has assaulted me, if that's what you mean.'

She looked searchingly into his brown eyes, so different from Luis' piercing black ones; they were kind, and he was genuinely concerned about her plight. She said quietly:

'Esteban, please answer me truthfully. Have you ever doubted that Peter was your brother's son?'

'Of course not,' he said without hesitation. 'Why should I?'

'Because Jo wrote to say he was dead.'

'Oh, Joanna!' He shrugged his shoulders. 'We all know, begging your pardon, that she was irresponsible. She would say anything to spite Pedro because he found her out.'

'What happened, exactly?' Laurel asked. 'She would never say.'

'So you don't know? They had a row, to do with some diamonds—men do not give diamonds for nothing. He threatened to take the baby away from her, so she bolted, presumably with her jet-set lover, and my brother was frantic about the fate of the child. Interpol traced the man to the Middle East, but she was not with him and he denied being implicated. She could have been anywhere between Spain and Timbuktu. Then that letter came postmarked London, so we assumed he had abandoned her there, having smuggled her in somehow—most things are possible if one has enough money. You had moved without leaving an address, and Pedro was going to London to seek verification when he was killed. Mama was ill and the matter fell into abeyance.'

'Until I wrote saying I was bringing the boy. That must have given you a nasty shock.'

'No, *querida*, a delightful surprise.'

'You're telling me! And you let me come without mentioning Jo's letter. That first afternoon you were all watching me, weighing me up, without giving a hint of your suspicions! Oh, now I come to think of it, Mercedes was muttering away in Spanish.'

'Being Mercedes, she had suggested you were trying to con us, but as soon as we saw you, we knew you were incapable of deceit. You are as different from your sister as gold from brass.'

'Thank you, but Luis was not convinced. Oh, it would have been so much more honest to have come out with it at once, instead of waiting all these weeks . . .' Her voice broke, and she covered her face with her hands.

'*Querida,*' gently he removed them, holding them in his. Luis need not have mentioned Joanna's wretched letter—it was bound to distress her. That and Cristina's presence next door, since she had this unfortunate fancy for his brother, which was probably the root of her trouble. He went on: 'I am not blind. I saw there was something between you and Luis at Ronda . . .' (she flinched). 'You both seemed lost in a dream, and I tried to warn you. You did know he was going to marry Cristina?'

'Yes, I knew,' she answered tonelessly.

'I am sure Luis did not want to hurt you, he is not a cad, though a little spoilt by feminine adulation, he thought you knew the score.'

'It's not that, Esteban.' She hadn't known the score, nor that Luis, that cruel devil was leading her on and on ... waiting to catch her out.

She withdrew her hands and in an expressionless voice told him what Luis had said to her that morning. With her hands folded in her lap, her eyes fixed upon a colourful cascade of nasturtiums falling over the wall in front of them, she kept nothing back, except the one thing that would have given a clue to Luis' attitude, her fictitious involvement with another man. As it was untrue, it did not seem to her to be important, and she was unaware of the fierce sexual jealousy she had aroused in Luis which had caused him to accuse her of being a liar and a cheat who had disowned her own child. That was the only deception she had practised, and it seemed so trivial compared to what he had done to her.

Esteban was completely bewildered. He loved and admired his brother and could not believe he would ever be deliberately cruel to any woman, even if Laurel was guilty of fraud, which he was certain she was not. Nor could he credit that Luis really thought so. He knew his mother and sister were very uneasy about his apparent yen for Laurel.

'*Querida*, I do not understand all this,' he protested. 'It is so unlike Luis to make such a monstrous allegation upon such flimsy evidence.' He brightened. 'But he will go to England, he will discover the truth ...'

Laurel interrupted feverishly: 'I don't want to stay here until he does . . . if he ever does. He has no right to *order* me to stay, which he did. I'd like to go now, at once, before he comes back,' for the hotel had become hateful to her. She turned big beseeching eyes upon Esteban. 'Will you help me?'

She was obviously overwrought, and he said soothingly:

'Of course I will, but what about the *niño*?'

Luis had promised Peter would not be victimised, and about that she trusted him. Though he might try to prevent him obtaining ownership of the Toro Negro, he would make provision for him.

'The break had to come,' she said sadly. 'Now would be a good opportunity. Luis has taken him down to the coast and he'll be too tired when he gets back to ask for me. In the morning you can tell him I was suddenly called away. You need not tell him I'm never coming back.'

'Never?'

'To return would only unsettle him.'

Esteban frowned, studying her pale, strained face. He thought Laurel had been exaggerating, she had misconstrued what Luis had said. Girls when emotionally upset did tend to make quartern loaves out of bread sticks, though Laurel normally seemed so sensible.

Cristina had been complaining that Luis was neglecting her, and he had been remiss. If that was because Laurel was distracting him, it boded no good for either of them. It might be better for all concerned if she did go, but he would miss her. He sighed.

'*Bueno*, Laurel, I am at your service. What do you want me to do?'

'Lend me my fare, I'll repay you as soon as I can. I'll get a taxi to Malaga.'

Esteban, who had never gone short of anything in his life, stared at her in astonishment. 'You mean you have no money?'

'Only what I earn, and I haven't been able to earn anything here. I was promised my return fare, but . . . I haven't been given it yet. Oh, Luis did give me some pocket money . . .' she faltered, as she recalled that evening in his room. Twice she had nearly succumbed, and despising her as he did, Luis would not scruple to use her to satisfy his lust. Lust, that was all he had ever felt for her, it had been stronger even than his contempt, but she . . . had loved him.

'All that I have is yours,' Esteban declared extravagantly. 'I will drive you to Malaga, I will come with you to England.'

'No, dear, you mustn't do that. Luis said once my sister had caused enough havoc in your family without me adding to it. They'd think we'd eloped.'

'That would be a wonderful idea!'

Laurel who was recovering slowly from her first despair had to laugh.

'It isn't at all. It would be Joanna and Pedro over again, with the difference that you don't love me and I don't love you. You're a wonderful friend, Esteban, but I couldn't accept such a sacrifice.'

'It would not be a sacrifice at all, but perhaps you are right. I am not quite ready for matrimony yet, but I hate to think of you alone in that grey, dreary city without support.'

'I managed before, and I'll manage again,' Laurel assured him. 'I'll get my things together and then perhaps we can be off?'

'As soon as you please.'

Laurel hesitated. 'You'll be kind to Peter?'

'Have I ever been anything else?' He grinned impishly. 'I will look forward to seeing Luis' face when he finds the bird has flown!'

Laurel turned her head away. 'Please don't talk about Luis.'

Esteban gave her a worried look. He did not like this hurried departure, but the girl had been badly hurt, perhaps it would be best for her to go before more harm could be done.

'I will bring my car to the main entrance,' he told her. 'As for repaying your air fare, do not consider that. It is owed to you, and I shall be reimbursed. But you may not be able to get a seat.'

'Then I'll wait at the airport until there's one available. There are often last-minute cancellations.'

Laurel hurriedly packed her case. When she came to the little box containing the withered rose, she threw it into the waste paper basket. She wanted no memento of Ronda.

She was fortunate, there was a spare seat on the London plane leaving in a couple of hours' time. Esteban insisted she must eat something, but she was not hungry, though she was glad of some coffee. When her flight was called, she told him:

'I'll be eternally grateful for what you've done for me. Just one more thing, don't tell Luis where I've gone.'

Instinctively she wanted to cover her tracks, though she had no reason to suppose anyone would want to find her.

'But if he asks?'

'You don't know. You weren't here when I left.'

'If that is the way you want it. I shall be glad to plead ignorance. Luis is not going to be pleased.'

'As pleased as a cat whose mouse has escaped,' she said bitterly. 'Oh, don't say any more about it,' as he seemed about to protest. 'I must go.'

As they reached Passport Control, he asked:

'You will let us know how you are faring?'

With whom should she communicate? His mother, who was jealous of her influence over Peter? Mercedes? That would be a laugh. Himself? She knew how that would be interpreted, and he would soon forget her among his bevy of girl-friends. Luis? God, no! She never wanted to have anything to do with him again.

'When I'm settled, I'll send Peter some postcards,' she told him.

Esteban looked dissatisfied. She looked so lost

and forlorn. 'If you are ever in any difficulty . . .'

'I'm sure I won't be,' she interrupted. She would not ask the Aguilas for help if she were starving.

'Ah, well,' he brightened. 'When all this mess is cleared up, Luis will get in touch with you, he will want to make amends.'

A stiff note of apology perhaps, which she could do without. He would have to be circumspect now he was becoming formally engaged to Cristina.

Her flight was called again.

Esteban kissed her gently. '*Vaya con Dios,*' he said huskily.

Go with God. She would need to ask for divine protection as she could not claim it from any man.

The plane rose high in the heavens, bearing her away from Andalusia, the flowers and scents of Mijas, and the love she had found and lost.

CHAPTER NINE

Upon her return to London, Laurel found refuge
at her old home, the St Agnes' Foundation, which
was always ready to provide temporary accommo-
dation to former inmates who were in difficulties.
The warden liked to keep in touch with them,
and in answer to her phone call told her to come
along and he and his wife would shelter her until
she could find lodgings. Laurel liked his choice of
words. 'Shelter' was what she needed, and the
grimy building in a north London square was the
only place she could call home.

St Agnes' had been endowed by a rich phil-
anthropist to be an orphanage for destitute girls.
It had originally been two large houses, and was
still divided into two sections, one for the under-
fives, the other for the school age girls. Attempts
had been made to modernise it from time to time
and introduce advanced ideas, like the breaking
up of the children into groups or families, but
shortage of funds and inadequate staff, consisting
mainly of young trainee nurses, who were more
interested in boy-friends than their charges, had
produced poor results. The children were well fed
and clothed, which was the main thing. Though
foster-parents are considered a better idea than
an institution, there were always more children

than people willing to foster. The warden and his wife were a kindly, dedicated couple, and Mrs Carter had always favoured the Lester girls, who were so pretty and for the most part docile, though Joanna was liable to tantrums. Several couples had wanted to adopt one of them, but she thought it would be cruel to part them, and nobody had been ready to take them both. Laurel had kept contact with them until Joanna had come back from Spain and then perforce had severed the connection.

Laurel gave the good lady an expurgated account of the past three years, but she could not conceal the fact that Joanna had left her husband. Mrs Carter thought that was understandable, mixed marriages were always a mistake. She was very sorry to hear of Joanna's death, and it was a comfort to know Peter was being well provided for. Privately she thought the Aguilas had treated Laurel very shabbily, turning her adrift after her care of him.

Upon contacting her old firm, Laurel was told regretfully that they had been unable to keep her job open, in fact they were cutting down staff. She visited an agency and the employment exchange, but it seemed likely she would have to subsist upon Social Security for an indefinite period, with far too much leisure to think.

It was then that Mrs Carter suggested she might like to work in the home. They were short-staffed, as the employment was not popular— 'Too much to do for too little pay,' she explained

wryly. Laurel would have her keep, her own bedroom and a small wage, until she could find
something better. Laurel accepted gratefully, and
her days became full with feeding, bedding and
superintending a variety of infants, many of whom
were black. She was not averse to scrubbing
floors, a perpetual chore, her object being to be
so occupied she had no time for brooding. At
night she was so exhausted she tumbled into bed
and was asleep as soon as her head touched the
pillow.

Upon sober reflection, she began to doubt very
much if in his heart of hearts Luis had really
believed Peter was her child. Egged on by his
sister, he had tried to make himself do so, for the
same reason that she had invented James Baron,
to combat the primitive urge in both of them that
was always seeking to draw them together. That
he had no prejudice against the boy himself was
significant, but he meant to marry Cristina
Ordoñez, so had sought to raise an impenetrable
barrier between them, and by making himself
believe she was despicable, could eliminate her
from his thoughts.

Perhaps she should have stayed as she had been
bidden to await the outcome of his investigations,
presumably he would have had the grace to
apologise, but he was not a man who would enjoy
having to abase himself, and an apology would
not have done much towards soothing her
outraged feelings. She would have had to leave
Mijas eventually, and she was glad that by enlist-

ing Esteban's aid, she had managed to get away without any more distressing scenes.

She had told Esteban not to say where she had gone, but Luis would know there was only one place where she could go, and she did not flatter herself he would look for her, even to make amends, no need to stir things up again, since she had passed out of his orbit, and by her own action. Nevertheless, she caught herself agog every time the telephone went and a visitor came to the door. But as the days passed and nothing happened, she ceased to be on the alert.

She sent picture postcards to Peter, views of the Tower, the Houses of Parliament, and colourful ones of the Horse Guards. Eventually she received a reply, a note in Doña Elvira's elegant script:

Dear Tia,

Thank you for the cards which I liked very much. Fifi is going to have pups. Lots of love.

and signed by himself in sprawling capitals: 'PEDRO.'

So Peter Lester was no more, and Pedro de las Aguilas had taken command. It was the only communication from Mijas that she did receive.

Laurel carefully refrained from visiting their former doctor or any of the sources which Luis might contact in his search, mindful of his last cruel stab. He might have let her know that she had been vindicated, she thought resentfully, but he might have been incensed by her flight, and think she deserved to be kept in ignorance, or maybe he had let the matter slide for the time being, his time begin occupied with preparations for his marriage. They would have the record of the birth of Pedro Lester de las Aguilas, if they couldn't find a death certificate, and it would be a long time before Peter came of age.

Summer passed into autumn and one bright morning with a touch of frost in the air, Laurel having gone on an errand found herself in the vicinity of the block of flats where she had lived with Joanna. On impulse she went to have a look at it. The tenants in her old flat had put up smart new curtains in the windows, and the building had been repainted, as if it wanted to eradicate all memory of the Lester sisters. She stood on the pavement thinking about poor Jo. Esteban had confirmed the truth about her, but she felt no blame, only pity for the foolish, feckless woman who had made such a mess of her life. She had been so lovely, but her beauty had been her bane, that silvery fairness that had enchanted the impressionable Pedro, and the other dark lover at Marbella. If only she had not written that lying letter that had ricocheted so unpleasantly upon herself, or at least told her sister what she had done so that Laurel could have explained its information was false, before turning up in Spain with a suspect child. Then Luis could have made his enquiries beforehand, and that shattering scene by the swimming pool need never have occurred.

A woman came along the pavement carrying a

shopping bag, and seeing her, exclaimed:

'Well, I never, if it isn't Laurel Lester! How are you, my dear?'

It was Mrs West, her neighbour in the old days who lived in the flat above the one she had rented.

Laurel explained that she had come back after leaving Peter in Spain, for Mrs West knew all about that, had in fact attended Joanna's funeral. The good woman seemed to have something on her mind, and insisted that Laurel should come in with her and have a cup of tea. Pleased to see a friendly face, Laurel agreed. Over their steaming cups, she told Mrs West as much as was good for her about Peter and Mijas, and how well he was settling down with his Spanish relations.

The flat, similar to the one below, comprised two rooms, bathroom and kitchenette, and was furnished in Victorian style with pieces from her former home. Mrs West was an ageing widow. There was Nottingham lace at the windows, small tables with bric-à-brac on them and an aspidistra in a pot, in front of the windowsill. The sight of its glossy green leaves recalled the ones in the hotel, though it was a far cry from this over-crowded little room to the Reina Isabella's marble vestibule, and Laurel faltered in her recital as she caught sight of it.

Her hostess refilled her thin china cup and looked at her compassionately.

'Bit of a wrench parting with the kiddie when you'd practically brought him up, but you'll be going out to see him, I don't doubt.'

Laurel said vaguely that she might do, knowing very well that she would not.

'And that reminds me, I'd almost forgotten, but seeing you brought it back to me. Some weeks ago I had a visit from a foreign gentleman ... very nice he was too though I was a bit chary about letting him in, there's some funny characters about nowadays, but he said he'd known Joanna out in Spain, and didn't she used to live in this block.'

Laurel tensed. 'Didn't he know she was dead?'

'Didn't seem to, but of course I told him. I know your sister always kept to herself, like, but seeing as she's gone I didn't think it mattered talking about her, and he did ask a lot of questions, mostly about the little boy.' Mrs West looked a little conscience-stricken. 'Somehow he led me on. Oh, but he was that nice, so sympathetic about my rheumatism, said I ought to winter in Ada ... Ada-something. It's the damp here that's so bad for it.'

Trying to make the question casual, Laurel asked what he had looked like.

'Oh, tall, dark and handsome, romantic hero type, though I like fair men best myself. My poor George was fair.' She looked anxiously at Laurel. 'Did I do wrong, dear, to talk so much? You know how it is when you're on your own all the time, your tongue does run away with you.'

Shame on you, Luis, for pretending you didn't know Jo was dead and pumping a garrulous old

woman. I suppose Peter told you our old address.
Laurel said slowly:

'I don't mind. What else did you tell him?'

'How brave you were, coping with the kiddy's
illness and then your sister's decline. Oh, I sang
your praises loud and long! I always was struck
with the way you shouldered your double burden
and kept your job at the same time. I told him too
how Peter used to come up here when he was
convalescing so I could keep an eye on him when
he was too much for his ma. Little monkey he
was too; shame there weren't no other children
for him to play with.'

'Your visitor must have found all this very
edifying,' Laurel remarked. 'Did he tell you his
name?'

'Said I'd never get my tongue round it and I
could call him Mr Lewis.'

Luis the sleuth, Laurel thought. Mrs West was
looking anxious.

'I hope I didn't bore him, but he seemed really
interested in everything I told him. I said as how
I hadn't had word nor sign of you since the day
you left, and had he run across you. But he told
me Spain was a big country and it was unlikely he
would.'

A neat get-out, Laurel thought. She was de-
riving a melancholy pleasure from Mrs West's
conversation. She could imagine Luis sitting where she was sitting, being oh, so suave
and charming—while he probed into her past history, the wretch. But Mrs West's next question

caused her to stiffen.

'You never knew a fellow called . . . what was it? James something, did you?'

'No. How did that come up?'

'I think he said they were mutual acquaintances, and they discovered he, this other chap, had met you and Joanna. Perhaps it was someone from your office?'

Oh, Luis, you . . . devil!

'Might have been, but I don't recall a James Baron.'

'Oh, yes, that was the name.' Mrs West looked at her sharply. 'So you had met him?'

'Must have done, somewhere, some time, or I wouldn't remember the name,' shrugged Laurel.

As if she could ever forget it! Had her phantom lover followed her to England?

'Well, anyway, I told him as you didn't have no boy-friends, never went out with anyone, didn't have time.'

What had Luis made of that?

Laurel thanked her hostess for the tea, made a few banal remarks and said she must go. Out in the street she made her way back to St Agnes', deep in thought. So Luis had been to London and had pursued his enquiries with a thoroughness she would have expected of him. Mrs West's innocent revelations must have been enlightening, and that chatty lady had told him she had not seen her since her return so he could not accuse her of complicity. How clever of him to pretend his interest was in poor old Jo, and how mean of him to bring up James Baron! She had nearly tripped up over that herself; if only she had never invented the creature. Some weeks ago, Mrs West had said, so he had come and gone without contacting herself. The address on her cards to Peter would have told him where she was living now, and he might have called to tell her she had been exonerated. He would be angry with her because she had run away from Mijas when he had told her to stay put, and would imagine she was busy getting herself engaged to James, but all the same . . . Oh, what was the use of expecting anything from him? She had gone out of his life and he did not mean to allow her to re-enter it.

She reached the home, opened the front door and went into the maelstrom of howling children and scolding staff. This was her life now. Coming back to St Agnes' had recalled vividly her teenage years and Jo. She had often had to cover up for her sister, even then, for Joanna was always getting into some foolish scrape. The wheel had turned full circle and she was back where she had begun. The interim years were fast taking on the unreality of a dream. Laurel went into the kitchen to don an apron and help with the children's teas.

About a week later, Laurel had just finished loading the dishwasher after midday dinner, when someone shouted to her: 'D'ye mind answering the front door, Laurel if you're not busy, there's someone ringing the bell fit to bust it.'

As if anyone at St Agnes' was ever not busy!

Without bothering to remove her apron, she wiped her work-roughened hands on a towel, pushed her straggling hair out of her eyes, and went to the door. Probably it was only some travelling salesman, or no one at all. Urchins often rang the bell and ran away—their idea of a joke. Feeling hot and tired, she drew back the latch and pulled it open, only to recoil in astonishment, for immaculate in grey suit, blue shirt, dark tie, was Luis de las Aguilas.

'Is Miss Lester available?' he asked pleasantly. 'I would like to speak to her.' He did a double-take. 'Laurel!'

Laurel felt a great surge of emotion at this unexpected sight of him. Involuntarily her hands went out to him and he took them in his, drawing her towards him. She had forgotten the pain of their last encounter, the insults he had heaped upon her, remembering only that she loved him and had longed for him to come and find her.

Luis eyes were glowing, and for a moment it seemed as if he were going to embrace her in the open doorway of St Agnes', in full view of the people in the street. Then he dropped her hands as if they were red-hot and the light went out of his eyes like a switched off lamp.

Laurel became aware of her bedraggled appearance which must have revolted him. Her apron was not clean, under it she was wearing the shapeless grey dress that was doled out to the staff as a kind of uniform, her hair was a mess and she wore no make-up, she had no time for such frivolities during her working hours, and there was probably a smut on her nose.

'*Nombre de Dios*, what have you done to yourself?' Luis demanded.

A good question, more correctly it was what he had done to her.

'Nothing. I'm working for my living,' she retorted.

He took in the dingy passage with its row of children's coats, the vinyl-covered floor; the pervading smell of stale food caused his aristocratic nose to wrinkle.

'Here?'

'Yes, here.' She looked at him defiantly. 'It's very worthy work, very necessary, very rewarding.'

She was babbling, thrown off balance. She had forgotten how good-looking he was, Prince Charming invading Cinderella's kitchen, and her heart was beating wildly. Somewhere an infant howled.

'I am sure it is,' he observed drily. 'Laurel, I have to speak to you. Is there somewhere private?'

Had he come to make a belated apology at last?

Silently she led the way into Mrs Carter's sitting room where visitors were usually received. Once a gracious room, it had acquired the institutional touch and needed redecorating, but there were two fairly comfortable armchairs. She indicated one of them.

'Please sit down.' She was struggling to untie

her apron, but of course the string had to be knotted. 'How is everyone? Is Peter all right?'

At last the apron was free and she folded it up hastily.

'It is about Pedro I have come.'

Alarmed, her confusion forgotten, she demanded: 'Has something happened to him? Is he ill?'

'I am afraid he is very poorly.'

She should not have left him, he hadn't been looked after properly. She whispered: 'Not . . . not dead?'

'Oh no, not as bad as that. Sit down, Laurel,' and as she made no move, he took her arm and propelled her into one of the armchairs.

'*Pequeña*, there is nothing of you, you are mere skin and bone!' He looked genuinely concerned.

'Never mind about me. Tell me about Peter.'

'He had to have an emergency operation for appendicitis. He came through all right, but he is not recovering as he should. It is still hot in Malaga where he is in hospital, and he asks continually for Tía to come and cool him.' Luis looked straight into her eyes. 'A memory, I believe, of his previous illness when you nursed him through measles and 'flu.'

He was telling her obliquely that he had confirmed the truth of her story, but Laurel did not care about that now, her whole mind was concentrated upon Peter.

'I must go to him,' she declared, twisting the apron in her hands, thinking of the miles of sea and land that separated her from the boy. 'Somehow.'

'Of course you must,' Luis told her briskly. 'I have come to fetch you. I hope your passport is up to date?' She nodded. 'I have a hired car outside to take us to Gatwick. How soon can you be ready?'

Mrs Carter came bustling in.

'Okay, Laurel, you can go now.' She glanced at Luis. 'Would you be the gentleman who rang up about an adoption?'

'I am afraid not, madam. I have come to borrow your assistant.' He explained about Peter.

'But if the child's had the operation, he'll soon be better,' Mrs Carter protested. 'Children are very resilient, and it's a long way to go if it isn't really necessary.'

She had found Laurel's services extremely useful and was loath to part with her. She hoped to make of her in time a dedicated worker like herself.

'You know we're in the middle of a staff crisis,' she went on. 'You can't really be spared.'

But staff crises were perennial at St Agnes'.

'Oh, I *must* go,' Laurel protested.

'Though the boy is her sister's child, Laurel has always been like a mother to him,' Luis said quietly, thereby conveying that he knew the truth. 'I assure you, madam, her presence is necessary for both their sakes.'

'Oh, very well,' Mrs Carter sighed resignedly. 'How long will you be away?'

Luis answered for her. 'Two or three weeks, depending upon the boy's progress.' He looked fixedly at Laurel. 'I see Pedro still comes first with you, though I know you have other commitments.' He didn't mean the Home, though Laurel was too perturbed to notice that. His eyes went from her face to her left hand, as though he expected to see a ring there. He went on: 'As soon as Pedrillo can be moved you shall take him up into the mountains, Laurel, where it will be cooler and you look as though you could do with some mountain air yourself. You can stay at the Toro Negro in Ronda.'

'The what?' Mrs Carter asked.

'It's a hotel,' Laurel told her, wishing Luis had suggested somewhere else. 'Luis owns about a dozen and uses them like weekend cottages.'

'Dear me!' Mrs Carter looked from one to the other, noting that Laurel had used the visitor's first name, but incredible as it seemed, he was one of poor Joanna's in-laws, though Laurel had omitted to introduce him. If her husband had looked like this one, why on earth had the little fool run away from him?

'Well, come back as soon as you can,' she said grudgingly. 'But after all, I can't expect to keep you for ever. You'll be leaving us when you get married.'

For unfortunately a girl with Laurel's looks was bound to marry some time.

Luis' face closed up like a clam and he looked at his watch pointedly.

'Will you please hurry, Laurel, or we will miss the plane.'

'I'll be as quick as I can.'

Laurel raced up the three flights of stairs to her attic bedroom. Looking at herself in the glass, she saw she had got a smut on her nose . . . and—oh heavens, her hair! She could not have presented a less glamorous appearance when she opened the door to Luis if she had tried. Not surprising he had jibbed at kissing her, for she was sure he had been going to do so, when he had taken her hands. But none of that mattered now in the face of Peter's need. She tore off her uniform dress, wishing she had time for a bath. In cord trousers, sweater and pseudo-suede coat, she looked more presentable. She threw what she thought she would need into her suitcase, which was still more battered than when she had hauled it off the conveyor belt at Malaga in the spring. She was about to embark upon the journey which she had never expected to take again and with Luis of all people, who was so indifferent he had not bothered until now to let her know he had discovered his base suspicions were unfounded. He must have become officially engaged to Cristina by this time, and she wished he had not selected Ronda for Peter's convalescence, but supposed it was a logical choice. Would the roses be still in bloom?

CHAPTER TEN

RONDA was mild and sunny for the most part, cooled by fresh breezes off the sierras. Occasionally there were heavy rain storms and the Guadalevin had become more than a trickle, leaping over the rocks from the New to the Roman bridge in a flurry of white water. Often Laurel wondered what Luis had been going to say, after she had told him she had never slept with a man, and Esteban had come barging into the conversation. 'In that case . . .' That he must leave her alone? That she needed initiation? She would never know now. Ronda was cold in winter, she was told, and there would be snow on the mountains, but the winter was very short, and it had not yet started.

Tourists still came to the Toro Negro, but in fewer numbers. Laurel and Peter were lodged in a private suite overlooking the gardens, and in the pure air he was fast regaining health and strength. The halcyon days were numbered, for when he was judged fully recovered, he would return to Mijas and she would go back to St Agnes'. She existed in a state of pleasant melancholy, for Luis never came to visit them, lost in dreams of what might have been if Luis had not been a proud Spaniard, and she not Joanna's sister. Their only contact with the outside world was Doña Elvira's frequent phone calls, which were all about Peter, and Ronda was a place for dreaming, especially the old town, with its winding streets and ancient fortifications, where she wandered at will while Peter was resting.

Laurel had only needed to spend a few days in Malaga, until Peter was considered strong enough to stand the journey to Ronda. This was accomplished in a luxurious limousine, with a nurse in attendance and frequent stops for refreshment. As for the flight to Malaga, that had passed without incident, Luis being courteous but distant, their conversation only of Peter-Pedro, and most of the time she had dozed. He made no reference to their last meeting, nor did he mention either his family or Cristina, and she, with her mind wholly occupied with Peter, had not wanted to introduce any controversial subject.

Peter had greeted her with plaintive reproaches.

'Tia, you said you'd not go while I wanted you, and I wanted you awful bad when my tummy hurted.'

'I came as soon as I heard about it, darling, but I have to look after lots of other children with no mummies or daddies. They need me too.'

'But I'm the most important,' Peter declared with Aguilas arrogance. 'You'll stay until I'm well again?'

'Of course.' She was relieved to note he did not

expect her stay to be permanent.

She did not see Luis again after he had decanted her at her hotel, another Aguilas property. Doña Elvira was also staying there, so that she could visit Peter daily, and seemed glad of Laurel's company, when they were not at the hospital. Esteban, she told her, was in the States, learning how the Americans did it, and what they expected in return for their dollars when on holiday. Mercedes was immured in her convent.

'So, I am much alone,' she sighed, 'except for Pedrillo, and he will be going away to school when he is seven.'

Too young for boarding school, Laurel thought anxiously, but oviously he would need younger company than his grandmother. Because she was longing to hear him mentioned, she said:

'But you still have Luis?'

The Spanish woman waved her small pudgy hands expressively.

'He is here, there, everywhere. Never do I believe he will settle down.'

'But when he is married?' Laurel asked, and waited with bated breath for her reply.

'Luis,' Doña Elvira said despondently, 'seems averse to matrimony. I thought he was prepared to wed Cristina, but *ay de mi*, still there is no engagement.' She gave Laurel a veiled look. 'It would appear he has a mistress somewhere who is the obstacle. Cristina is sure of it.'

'Not guilty,' Laurel told her, with a forced laugh. 'I haven't seen your son since I left Mijas except for the journey here.'

The Señora looked at her doubtfully. 'He was in England for quite a long time.'

'I heard he'd been there from a mutual acquaintance, but I thought it was just a flying visit.' She stifled a pang. They had been in the same city, he for quite a long time, and he had not thought her worth a call.

'Then it must be that Manuelita Gomez in Torremolinos,' Doña Elvira declared. 'She is a flamenco dancer and half gypsy. All the men are crazy about her, the slut, and he may find the competition a challenge. Naturally she will give him preference.' She lifted her dark head, in which there was as yet no grey, proudly. 'My Luis is a king of men.'

A confidence Laurel would have preferred to do without. Cristina she had had to accept, but she knew it was not a love match; that Luis was involved elsewhere pained her. She pictured a sultry, sexy beauty in the glamorous flounced dress the dancers wore, who would have completely eliminated any lingering memory of Laurel Lester, who had become washed out and uninteresting in the service of others. She glanced at her toil worn hands lying in her lap, which had once been so white and smooth. She could have taken better care of them, but it had not seemed worth while.

'Won't you come with us to Ronda?' she had asked, thinking she would welcome the other woman's company now she seemed disposed to be friendly. She had already been told there would only be herself and Peter there.

'No, no, I do not like mountains, and the Casa will need my supervision.' She gave Laurel a half sly smile. 'You are a good, kind girl, Laurelita, and I always thought Joanna's letter was a lie, whatever Mercedes said. Luis received glowing reports of you from your friends.'

'But he never came to see me,' Laurel blurted out.

'Perhaps he had his reasons,' Doña Elvira had said enigmatically.

A fascinating flamenco dancer, how could goodness and kindness compete with her lure? Do-gooders were not sexually exciting, and when she met Luis again she had had a smut on her nose!

Two days after this conversation she had left for Ronda with Peter.

The gardens had an autumnal air, the agave blooms were over, the geraniums losing their petals, but there were still roses, a few dark red ones lingered on the bush whence Luis had picked one for Laurel. She knew now her love for him was still strong, neither his cruel accusations nor his neglect had killed it, that moment on the doorstep of St Agnes' had revived it, but she had looked a drab, and Luis had recoiled from her. It was only her looks that had attracted him, she thought drearily, he was not interested in the woman behind them. If he lost his, would she be similarly affected? She did not think so, he would be still Luis, the man she loved, and however disfigured he became, she would only love him all the more for what he had once been.

One day after they had been at the hotel for about a week, she and Peter were finishing their lunch, when a party was ushered into the restaurant with unctuous deference by the head waiter. It comprised a stout middle-aged couple, obviously husband and wife, another middle-aged man, with a fine head but a dissolute face, and Cristina. The Ordoñez family having a day out, or was Cristina expecting Luis would be there? Laurel hoped she would not be noticed, but Peter exclaimed loudly:

'There's Tio Luis' *novia!*'

Cristina turned to stare at them, and Laurel smiled mechanically, as she told Peter to hush.

'Finish your dessert, dear, it's time for your rest.'

The Ordoñez party having ordered, Cristina rose from her seat and came across to them.

'So you here again,' she said rudely.

She had put on a little weight, as her too tight suit revealed, and her eyes were unfriendly.

'Tia came because I've been ill,' Peter explained proudly. 'I had my tummy cut.'

Cristina glared at him. 'We all know that. Luis make more fuss of you than if you his own son, which . . .' She gave Laurel a glacial glance, 'perhaps you are.'

Laurel sighed. Peter's paternity apparently had opened up a fresh area of conjecture. If only he had been dark!

'Is Señor de las Aguilas here?' Cristina demanded, without giving Laurel time to say anything.

'No, and I've no idea where he is,' Laurel replied. 'Peter, I mean Pedro ...' Peter insisted upon the Spanish form of his name now, 'and I are here while he is convalescing. Señor de las Aguilas has not been here at all.'

'Tio Luis is too busy,' Peter supplemented.

Cristina looked unconvinced. Then she shrugged her plump shoulders. 'Send that brat away,' she commanded, 'I have something to tell you.'

Laurel sighed again, foreseeing an unpleasant interrogation, but she could not avoid it without being rude, and she had an unwilling curiosity to know the state of affairs between Luis and this girl, which Cristina probably meant to reveal.

'Shall we wait until you've had your lunch?' she suggested, 'I see your starters have arrived and I have to settle Pedro for his siesta. I will be at your service on the terrace, *señorita*.'

She had some difficulty in persuading Peter to rest. He was incensed at being called a brat, and he didn't want Cristina to be his tia. 'Tio Luis can't know how nasty she is,' he insisted, adding with perception beyond his years. 'But she's never nasty to him.'

When at length she was free, she went to sit among the white tables and chairs set out on a terrace facing the blue humps of the distant mountains beyond the garden. She ordered coffee and waited resignedly for the other girl to appear.

Eventually Cristina came, replete with a good lunch, waving her fan, and sat down opposite Laurel, eyeing her with hostility.

'You still run after Señor de las Aguilas?' she enquired insolently. 'You get nothing there. He never, never marry a slut out of an *orfelinato*.'

'There has never been any question of that,' Laurel told her with dignity. 'I've only seen Señor de las Aguilas once since I left Mijas and that was when he came to fetch me when Peter was in hospital. If you came up here expecting to find him with us, I'm afraid you've had a wasted journey. He hasn't been to Ronda while we've been here.'

Which had been disappointing. Laurel had thought he would find time to come and see how Peter was progressing, but he had not done so, nor, when she rang up, had his mother suggested he might be coming. Ronda without Luis was Eden without Adam, but at least she could face Cristina with a clear conscience.

Cristina stared at her belligerently, but the wistful expression on Laurel's face seemed to reassure her. She relaxed visibly.

'No see me either,' she said plaintively, and Laurel felt sorry for her. Luis had treated her very casually. 'He go to England,' Cristina went on, 'I think to find you. He come back, but he do not come to Sevilla. I am told you here, so I come, but no Luis.' She looked round as if expecting him to materialise in a puff of smoke like a pantomime demon. '*No comprendo.*'

'I'm sorry,' Laurel spoke gently. 'Do believe me that it isn't on my account Luis has been so neglectful. We haven't communicated since I left.'

'Ah!' A malicious gleam shone in Cristina's dark eyes. 'He get over his madness, so.' She closed her fan with a snap. 'Men fickle.'

'I always understood he was going to marry you.'

'Not now. I look for him to tell him I marry the Duque de Ortego y Montañero. Not rich like Luis, but I have title. Papa give me huge dowry. A *duque* much better than a hotel keeper.'

She looked at Laurel triumphantly.

Laurel recalled noticing the middle-aged roué in the dining room. Was that the duke? As a man he was a poor exchange for Luis. Cristina was assuaging her wounded pride with a title.

'Congratulations,' she said sincerely.

'*Gracias.*' She opened her fan again. 'Luis young girl's dream, but . . .' she shook her head sadly, 'him no good. I wait no longer.'

'I wish you every happiness,' Laurel said, and meant it.

'To be *duquesa* make me very happy.' Cristina nodded complacently. 'Luis at Mijas?'

'I've no idea.'

Cristina looked at her commiseratingly. 'You tired,' she said, and anxiety over Peter on top of toil at St Agnes' had quenched most of Laurel's sparkle. 'So Luis drop you.'

Laurel smiled wryly. 'He never picked me up.'

They became silent, looking over the garden to the distant mountains, both were recalling a vanished dream.

Finally Cristina stood up.

'I ring the Señora,' she said decisively. 'Maybe she tell me where to find Luis. I wish everyone to know of my betrothal.'

She held out her hand; now Laurel was no longer a rival she could afford to be sympathetic. They were both in a sense Luis' victims. Laurel took it, noticing the ruby bracelet on Cristina's wrist. Was that the duke's engagement token?

'*Adios, señorita,*' Cristina said graciously. She teetered away on her high heels to rejoin her duke. Laurel sat on watching the shadows lengthen. Luis' fancy for her had died, and he had abandoned Cristina for a gypsy dancer. As the Spanish girl had said: 'Men fickle.'

Dawned the morning of their last full day at Ronda. On the following one they would be leaving. The manager informed Laurel at breakfast that El Señor would be arriving to check the hotel's accounts and other business before noon. He would be engaged all day, and would spend the night. In the early morning he would take her and Peter back to Mijas. Transport would be provided for her from thence to Malaga, where a reservation had been made for her on the plane to London. Would this be satisfactory to the Señorita? The man was ill at ease, a visit from Luis was an ordeal for his staff, for any shortcomings would be severely reprimanded.

Laurel assured him the arrangements would suit her perfectly and watched him hurry away with some amusement. The advent of the big boss was causing a flutter in the dovecote and her own heart was fluttering too. Luis was coming at last, and though he might be busy all day, she would have the long drive back to Mijas beside him, a bittersweet pleasure with the recollection of their former journey to and from Ronda with no cloud between them except a shadowy Cristina. Now that had dispersed, but a gulf between them had opened, she had lost much of her good looks, and Luis was enamoured of a dancer in Torremolinos.

Peter was on the qui vive for his uncle's arrival, and dashed out to meet him when he saw the Silver Shadow coming down the avenue of palm trees that led to the hotel. He dodged other cars at considerable risk to life and limb, while Laurel watched anxiously from the hotel entrance, unable to intervene. With relief she saw them coming towards her, Peter hanging on Luis' arm.

'He is still alive,' was Luis' greeting. 'But I though that red car was going to get him. Does he often do that?'

'No, only for you.' She was glad of the diversion for her heart was beating madly. Luis had for once abandoned formal clothes and wore a black sweater above black cord pants. The garb suited him, outlining his lean, muscular frame.

'He was in a hurry to get to you,' she went on.

'He was afraid you'd disappear into the office without saying hello.'

'I am not in such great haste to become immersed in the hotel's discrepancies,' Luis returned, smiling. 'Shall we go outside and have a drink before I commence operations?'

He was as darkly magnetic as he had always been, in every fibre Laurel was aware of him, feeling herself come alive under the stimulus of his presence. Last time they had met, she could think only of the sick child, but today it was Luis who absorbed her. She was like a thirst-crazed desert wanderer who had found a spring of fresh water.

Peter answered in Spanish to the effect that that would be a lovely idea, and pranced on ahead. Luis watched him fondly.

'He is progressing with the language, and he has grown since his operation.' He held the swing door open for her to pass through on to the terrace, and his glance swept over her body. She wore brown slacks and a bright green blousette in soft piled bouchette fabric with a deep vee neck. She had lost most of her summer tan, but excitement at his coming had brought a wild rose tint to her cheeks. Her eyes were shadowed and she was much too thin. When they were seated, where she had sat with Cristina, he gave his order and then examined Peter critically.

'He looks very well,' he decided. 'Quite himself again.'

'I've still got a red mark on my tummy,' Peter told him, unwilling to discard the role of pampered invalid.

'You will always have a scar, but it will turn white.'

The waiter brought their refreshment very promptly, and he turned his regard upon Laurel.

'More than I can say for you. I hoped the fresh air up here would do you good. You are thin as a willow wand, and your eyes are like bruised pansies.'

She flushed and paled under his keen scrutiny.

'Oh, I'm all right. I've not been sleeping well, that's all.'

'Why is that?' he asked sharply.

Because I can't get you out of my thoughts and this place is redolent of you—but she could not tell him that. Instead she said:

'I've been worrying about how Mrs Carter is managing.'

'I do not think you are losing sleep over her,' he returned. 'She managed before you came to her. Be honest, Laurel, you are pining for your James, but you will soon be reunited.'

'Who's James?' Peter demanded.

'Has she not told you? Someone who is going to make your Tia very happy.'

'You don't mean she's going to get married?' He stared at Laurel aghast. 'Not some beastly English guy? I wanted her to marry a Spanish *hidalgo* so she would be here always. Why don't you marry her, Tio? That would be super.'

Peter's vocabulary was becoming a strange mixture of tongues.

'Your aunt does not trust Spaniards,' Luis said bitterly. 'She said she would only marry an Englishman.'

So she had—long ago, but here was one misconception she would remove before she left, Laurel decided.

'If you're talking about James Baron,' she said, 'there's no such person.'

' 'Course not!' Peter exclaimed triumphantly. 'I knew you'd got it wrong, Tio Luis, and I think that's a horrible name.'

'It was invented on the spur of the moment,' Laurel confessed.

Luis was sitting very still, his face inscrutable. Then he took out his car keys. 'Pedro, there is a parcel on the back seat of the Shadow wrapped in red paper. It is a present for you. Go and get it, and you can open it at once if you like.' He handed the boy the keys.

'I don't know if he can manage the lock.' Laurel rose to her feet, suddenly afraid of being alone with Luis.

' 'Course I can!'

Peter vanished like smoke, as Luis' hand clamped over Laurel's wrist.

'Stay where you are.' He looked up at her with reproachful eyes. 'Why, Laurel, in God's name why?'

She sank back on to her seat, her wrist still manacled by Luis' strong brown fingers.

'I needed some defence against . . .' she blushed vividly and stared down at the table '. . . you know what. You were engaged to Cristina and I . . . I couldn't become your mistress.'

'With the result you were never nearer to being raped in your life,' he retorted caustically. 'No, that is the wrong word—you were willing. That was a damn stupid thing to say. Laurel—to be told another man had got there first nearly drove me crazy, and I have never been engaged to Cristina.'

Laurel tried to free her wrist, but his grip tightened.

'Look at me,' he commanded.

Drawn by some force she could not resist, Laurel unwillingly raised her eyes. He stared into their limpid depths as he had so often done before.

'Virgin's eyes,' he said at length, and released her.

She rubbed her wrist against her trouser leg to restore the circulation.

'You didn't think so that morning by the pool,' she told him bitterly, 'when you accused me of being Peter's mother.'

'*Querida,*' his voice was very soft, 'you had been playing with fire. Did you not expect retaliation?'

'So that was what it was! I could call it slander, defamation of character and a few other things, and to round off your charming epithets, which amounted to liar and fraud, you said definitely you were going to marry Cristina. But that didn't come off, did it? She's thrown you over and latched herself on to a seedy duke.'

Not at all perturbed, Luis told her: 'I always knew

you had a temper. I like a woman with spirit. Yes, Cristina told me she has captured a duke and expected me to be overwhelmed with grief at the loss of her person . . . and her pesetas.'

'Which you weren't?'

'I pretended to be, to soothe her vanity, which was all that was hurt. After all, I had aroused her expectations. I *had* intended to marry her, but I could not bring myself to propose to her, not while my heart was longing for . . . you.'

'But you couldn't marry a slut out of an *orfelinato*, as she so politely told me.'

'When was this?'

'She came up here looking for you. She wanted to flourish her duke in your face. Nice lot, you Spaniards . . .' Laurel was very angry, he seemed quite unmoved by all the distress he had caused her . . . 'Because I very rightly tried to repel you, putting up the only defence I could think of, you put me through purgatory with your horrible insinuations, and Cristina sells herself for a title to spite you.'

'You are no better. You sent me to hell pretending you were involved with a non-existent suitor. I thought that was why you ran away from Mijas without waiting for my return. You had already told me, you little liar, you had been away from him too long. After that, I had to keep away from you. I dared not even visit you in London to offer my apologies, in case I found you with this James Baron—loathsome name!—for then I would have killed him.'

Peter was running towards them, waving red

wrapping paper in one hand, and grasping a toy replica of the Silver Shadow in the other. He caught the last words.

'Killed who?' he demanded with interest. 'Not the man who wants to marry Tia? She says he's not real.'

'Tia,' Luis said with great decision, 'is going to marry me.'

'Oh, goody!' But Peter at that moment was more excited by his present, than Laurel's matrimonial prospects. 'It's super, Tio Luis, thank you—I mean *gracias muchas*.'

'*Muchas gracias*,' Luis corrected him. 'And where are my car keys?'

'I left them in the lock of the car,' Peter said blithely.

'Then go and get them, *cretino*. You can leave your present here until you come back.'

'*Perdon*, Tio Luis.' Peter was off like a rocket and Luis turned to look at Laurel. She was gazing at him in wide-eyed astonishment.

'You can't mean that, Luis—me, an orphanage slut?'

'The finest little woman in the world, or so your friends tell me.'

Reminded of his duplicity, she said tartly: 'Yes, Mrs West gave me a good testimonial, didn't she? But prior to that . . .'

'I was well aware of your excellent qualities,' he interrupted, 'until I allowed Mercedes to play on my jealousy. I am afraid I am a jealous man, Laurelita. It is a part of loving . . . Oh, what *is* it?'

The manager had approached bowing deferentially, indicating in Spanish that all was ready for El Señor's inspection. At the same moment Peter returned with the car keys, and Luis groaned.

'You had better go and do your duty,' Laurel told him, 'and allow me time to collect myself.'

Had Luis been about to confess he loved her?

Resignedly Luis rose to his feet. 'And do not dare to run away,' he threatened, then his face softened. 'You and I have both suffered, but the best is still to come.'

As the two men walked away, Peter looked up from examining his toy, to enquire:

'You don't really mind Tio Luis being Spanish, do you, Tia? After all, I'm Spanish too.'

Laurel threw her arms round him and kissed him, much to his disgust.

'I love everything Spanish.'

'You go round like a weathercock,' Peter reproved her, 'but I only like being kissed when I'm ill.'

Luis had different ideas, but it was not until after dinner with Peter safely asleep that he was able to demonstrate how much he liked being kissed and kissing. They had wandered out into the gardens where a yellow moon had replaced the sun. The old magic was still there, the rapturous response, but Luis was gentle, his passion held in check. Presently he reluctantly released her, and with a hand under her chin, tilted her face so the light fell full upon it. The moon's rays turned her skin to ivory, her hair to silver, but her eyes were like stars.

'*Amada*,' he began earnestly, 'if you have any doubts express them now, and we will reconsider, for once we are married, I will never, never let you go.'

She answered steadily: 'I've loved you for a long time, Luis, and I'm ready to take a chance on you, but you must trust me, for when you called me a fraud you all but broke my heart.'

'For that I humbly beg your pardon, it was, as you might say the last ditch before my final defences crumbled. I nearly asked you to marry me on that day when we stood above the gorge, but ... well, we know what happened to your sister, and I felt we must make very sure, and you *were* a fraud when you trumped up James Baron. Then I saw red, I was ready to believe anything bad of you to get you out of my system.'

'But it didn't work?' she asked softly.

He shook his head. 'I could not oust you from my heart. When I saw you again on the doorstep of that unspeakable place, I longed to sweep you into my arms and carry you away, pamper you with luxury, do anything to make amends.'

'Me, with my hair like a bird's nest, and a smut on my nose?'

'Was there? To me you always looked lovely, and there was a light in your eyes ... but then that good lady talked about you getting married, and I thought I must have been mistaken.'

'She didn't mean anyone in particular, but she was afraid some man would take me away from her eventually. She was right. You wouldn't let me go back and work out a month's notice to placate her? She was very good to me when I had nobody else to turn to, and I was fond of the children.'

'Most certainly not. I will give the Home a large donation to compensate for your loss.' He drew her back into his arms. 'And if you want children perhaps I can do something about that.'

Laurel laughed, and snuggled against him, murmuring in his ear:

'Your mother did tell me something about a flamenco dancer in Torremolinos, but if I'm to be a good Spanish wife, I suppose I must look the other way.'

'Mama should not tell tales. I went to Manuelita seeking distraction when you seemed lost to me, but it was useless, she sickened me. There will never be anyone but you, *luz de mi vida*.'

Enlaced, they wandered on through the scented garden, not noticing the air was turning chill. Beside the rose bush from which he had once given her a blossom, Laurel stopped.

'Luis!'

'What is it now?'

'You haven't said it, you know.'

'Said what?' he sounded anxious.

'That you love me.'

'For now and for ever. All that I have is yours, including my heart.'

'You still haven't said it.'

And then he did, but it was in Spanish.

THE SPANISH NATIONAL DISH

A romance set in Spain wouldn't be complete without mention of *paella*, the Spanish national dish. If your taste runs to Spanish foods, you won't be disappointed with this saffron-flavored entrée.

What you need:

   2 cloves garlic, chopped
   1/4 cup olive oil
   3-4 lb. chicken, cut into pieces
   2 cups rice, uncooked
   2 tsp. saffron
   4 cups hot chicken stock
   1 cup peas
   2 sweet red peppers, sliced
   8 thin slices *chorizo* or other highly seasoned
      sausage
   12 raw shrimp
   12 clams in shells

What to do:

Preheat oven to 350°F. (176°C.). In a Dutch oven, lightly sauté garlic in olive oil over a moderate heat. Remove garlic. Brown chicken in same oil, remove and set aside. Add rice to oil and stir until lightly browned. Dissolve saffron in chicken stock, then add to rice. Mix in peas, peppers, sausage and chicken. Cover and bake for 30 minutes. Arrange shrimp and clams on top, then cover and return to oven for 10 minutes. Makes 6 to 8 servings.